Terror in Eagle Basin

CLIFF FARRELL

DOUBLEDAY & COMPANY, INC.

GARDEN CITY, NEW YORK

1974

All the characters in this book are fictitious, and any resemblance to actual persons, living or dead, is purely coincidental.

Library of Congress Cataloging in Publication Data

Farrell, Cliff.
    Terror in eagle basin.

    I. Title.
PZ4.F244Te   [PS3556.A766]   813'.5'4
ISBN 0-385-03096-7
Library of Congress Catalog Card Number 73–18911

Dedicated to the author's five grandsons

Terror in
Eagle Basin

CHAPTER ONE

It was early June, and the Aguila Mountains, which soared above the rugged southwestern desert, had enjoyed an unusual winter of ample rains. The rough slants were responding with luxuriant beauty. Blooming wild lilac festooned the darker chaparral. Purple lupine tried to soften the rocky hillsides. On the lower slopes, the plumes of the yucca stood sentinel duty over all of nature's wealth. White jewels decorated the manzanita, wild roses were offering small, graceful flowers, trying to match the incredibly delicate blooms on the cactus.

It was different with the stagecoach trail. It had been originally a part of the Butterfield route, which had been deserted years before when the Civil War erupted but was now reestablished as a link between Rimrock in the high country, and the transcontinental railroad on the desert below. Dan Cameron had boarded the stagecoach early that morning at a desert town named Aguila Junction, and it was now late afternoon of a day-long ordeal. The coach was an old Concord whose thoroughbraces had long ago lost all resilience. The wheels of the vehicle seemed to find every rock and thank-you-ma'am in the narrow tortuous ascent.

Dan Cameron, a long, lean-muscled man of twenty-eight, with Indian-dark hair and dark eyes, was wedged with two other men in the rear seat. Being more than a little acquainted with stagecoach journeys, he would have preferred the forward seat, where the inconvenience of riding backward was outweighed by the advantage of having support for one's back when the coach was pitching and yawing over the obstacles. However, he had deferred to the comfort of a Franciscan padre and a female who had also boarded at the railroad stop.

One of his seat companions was a burly, hard-mouthed, rough-mannered man who had stated that his name was Pete Slater. Slater had stripped off his coat and celluloid collar and traveled in a rather soiled striped shirt equipped with brass collar buttons. He did not shed the six-shooter that was holstered at his side.

With Slater was a fussy, irascible little man who had said his name was Abel Jenkins and that he was on his way back to his business in a town named Pinedale after a trip east. He was balding and round-bellied, with a rusty derby hat jammed on thinning, rusty hair. He and the driver, who evidently were old enemies, had been exchanging words that were growing increasingly bitter, for Abel Jenkins was blaming the man for the hardships of the journey.

The padre was a gray-templed, kindly-faced man in a threadbare knee-length coat and the white collar of his calling, and wore a round-crowned, flat-brimmed hat. He had said that he was returning to his parish after having attended a wonderful religious affair at Santa Fe, far to the east.

The padre's companion on the forward seat, evidently also wise to the facts of stagecoach travel, had chosen her place when given her choice at the start of the journey. Dan approved of her intelligence in this respect, but that was about all he could make out of her, for she obviously had no intention of falling into conversation with him or any of the others aboard. She wore an ankle-length linen dustcoat and had a dust veil over her bonnet, which was draped past her chin so that she could have been homely of feature or very fetching for all he knew. Or cared.

He still grieved deeply for the fair-haired, soft-voiced, soft-eyed girl who had married him only a few months in the past and who had died in his arms on their wedding day. That

2

love affair had been as tender as the bursting of spring, as warm as the bright days of summer, as dreamy as the coming of fall. And then sudden winter.

The coach swayed and seemed to hang perilously over space as it gave room for a downward-bound ore wagon on which driver and swamper hung to long brake poles. Dust swirled suffocatingly upon the coach passengers and the ordeal was repeated moments later when a high-sided wagon, loaded with the long sacks of wool from spring's shearing, edged past.

The coach surged ahead once again. Dan heard the leaders break step and he braced himself, knowing what was coming. The jolt struck, wheels clashed, and the coach lurched violently and righted itself.

Abel Jenkins was pitched forward against the padre's knees. Mumbling in a rage, he scrambled back into his seat only to again be toppled into the padre's arms.

That was the last straw for Jenkins. He half arose, clinging to the window ledge, thrust his head into the open, and screeched: "You brainless idiot! What are you trying to do, Coates, kill us all?"

It was not the first complaint Abel Jenkins had voiced. This time the coach came to an abrupt halt, and the brake was locked. The driver, whose name was Clem Coates, leaped to the ground and his tough face appeared at the side of the coach. He was a heavy-shouldered, heavy-featured man with the flattened nose and scars of a brawler. He yanked open the door of the coach. "You infernal weasel!" he snarled. "I've had enough of you an' yore bellyachin', Jenkins. As long as you don't like the way I handle my coach, you kin walk!"

He reached in, grasped the small man by the lapels of his coat, and dragged him bodily out of the coach. He brought a big hand down on the derby hat, jamming it around the ears of his victim.

Abel Jenkins was outweighed by forty pounds, and no

match in strength with the driver. But there was a ratlike viciousness in him, and he fought with frenzied ferocity.

He twisted his head around and screeched, "Slater!" He was addressing the collarless man alongside Dan. Pete Slater started to reach for his six-shooter, evidently intending to shoot Clem Coates in the back, but Father Terence O'Flaherty leaned across the narrow space and gripped Slater's arm, preventing him from drawing.

"There's no need for gunplay, me boy," the priest said.

Clem Coates was manhandling his tormentor. He slapped Jenkins in the face with an open palm, then whirled him around and kicked him, sending him sprawling in the dust. He moved to continue his attack.

"Stop him!" It was the veiled passenger who had spoken.

Dan realized that he was the one she was addressing. He felt that angry eyes were on him through the veil. "Aren't you going to do *anything?*" she demanded when Dan did not move. "That little man hasn't a chance against that bully."

"It isn't my fight," Dan said.

The breeze momentarily lifted the veil and he had a glimpse of very scornful hazel-green eyes and a comely chin and mouth. "That's the easy way out, isn't it?" she exploded.

She gathered her skirts and leaped through the open door to the ground. She was lithe and agile. "Stop it!" she cried, overtaking the burly driver and his victim. When Clem Coates did not immediately respond, she snatched off his sweat-stained hat, grasped his thick, greasy hair, set her heels in the dust, and yanked.

Coates uttered a yelp of injury. He abandoned his quarry and whirled, his ugly face stormy. "You git back in thet coach an' mind yore own business, whoever you air, lady!" he snarled. "This little rabbit is goin' to walk the rest o' the way to Rimrock."

"If anyone is going to walk it'll be you!" she panted.

Clem Coates was standing on the shoulder of the road, which dropped away down a long rocky slope to a dry gully two hundred feet below. Before he realized his danger, the young woman placed her hands against his chest and gave him a shove with all her strength.

Coates uttered a howl of dismay, but too late. He reeled backward, then went tumbling head over heels down the slant, riding a small avalanche of loose earth.

The young lady brushed her hands. "Get aboard!" she snapped, addressing Abel Jenkins. The rotund little man, dusty, enraged, glared down at Clem Coates as though considering continuing the fight, then thought better of it and scrambled aboard.

"Can you drive?" the young lady demanded. "Have you ever handled a six?"

Dan discovered that a stabbing forefinger was pointed at him. He shrugged. "I'd prefer to keep out of this, ma'am," he said.

He saw that he was being surveyed from the toes of his soft-bench-made boots to the top of his creased, wide-brimmed range hat. He sensed that back of the veil her scorn was considerable.

She glanced down into the gully, where Clem Coates was dazedly trying to get to his feet. Apparently all that had been injured was his dignity. "You're afraid of that catawampus," she said caustically.

"Could be," Dan said.

She glared at the padre and at Pete Slater and decided she would get no help there. "All right," she said grimly.

She gathered her skirts, and before Dan or the other men could protest, mounted the box, picked up the reins of the six-horse team, and began trying to arrange them.

"Lady!" Pete Slater croaked, "you ain't intendin' to try to *drive*, air you?"

"I certainly am," she said. "If any of the rest of you prefer to walk, now's the time to say so."

"How far is it to Rimrock?" Dan asked.

"Four, maybe five miles," she said.

"I'm no good at walking," Dan said. "But how good are you at handling this?"

"You'll find out," she snapped. She released the brake. "Hike!" she shouted at the team.

The surprised horses jumped into motion, and the coach lurched ahead. It promptly bounced through a chuckhole and skidded, and the hubs scraped a trailside boulder. Dan feared for a moment that it was going to capsize.

"She's no better at it than Clem Coates," Abel Jenkins moaned.

"I heard that," she shouted from above.

There were distant, profane sounds. Clem Coates was trying to scramble back to the road, yelling threats that were spiced with brimstone.

Pete Slater tried to open a door, intending to leap from the coach, but Abel Jenkins pushed him back. "No you don't!" he chattered. "If I stay, you stay. It's me that's payin' you to stick with me."

Dan realized that the horses were out of control. He opened the opposite door, reached up, seized the baggage railing, and managed to pull his six-foot length to the roof. The girl was clinging desperately to the reins, trying to slow down the animals.

Dan scrambled to the seat, pushed her aside and took over the reins. It was touch-and-go for a time, but he finally brought the horses under discipline and they settled down to their routine gait.

The girl drew a sigh of relief. "I guess I took on a little more than I could handle," she admitted. "I didn't figure on that big off horse in the swing team being so rank. He's the one who spooked the others."

"What's your name?" Dan asked. "Not that it matters."

"Spring," she said. "Jennifer Spring."

"Wait until Clem Coates catches up with you," Dan said.

"Fiddlesticks!" she sniffed. "That big bully. I hope he grows a nice crop of blisters."

"Do you live in Rimrock?"

"No. I expect to live in Eagle Basin. That's another day's ride beyond Rimrock. Fifty miles or so. Speaking of Rimrock, there it is ahead. We were closer than I realized."

The roofs of the town were visible ahead through the scattered pines of the high country. The sun was low in the west, painting the false fronts and walls of Rimrock in hues of gold and bronze. The town was bigger than Dan had anticipated. It was a county seat, dominated by the clock tower of a courthouse, built in the baroque fashion of all public buildings. The coach topped a rise, and Dan saw that the court building stood in a plaza shaded by maples and pines in a background of green lawn.

The town was surrounded by a green pine forest. The head frame of a silver mine jutted from the trees on a ridge beyond the town. Sheep wagons and ore wagons were parked in back lots. It was cooler here with the heady fragrance of hayfields in the sundown air. It should have been sedate and peaceful at this approaching supper hour, but Dan saw that the place was an anthill as he tooled the stage into the head of the principal street.

Cow ponies and settlers' wagons crowded the hitchrails along the street. The courthouse plaza was thronged, but the remainder of the street seemed deserted.

Dan located the stagecoach office near the head of the street. It was flanked by a wagonyard, corral, and barn. He swung the coach through the open gate into the yard and brought the horses to a stop. Abel Jenkins and Pete Slater lost no time in alighting and went hurrying toward the courthouse.

A hostler who had been standing on the sidewalk gazing in that direction came reluctantly into the yard. He stared blankly at Dan. "Who air you?" he demanded, peering around.

7

"The name is Cameron," Dan said. "I'd like to have my luggage from the boot now. Could you direct me to the Stockade Hotel? It's been recommended to me."

"Whar's Clem?" the hostler gurgled. "Clem Coates?"

Jennifer Spring answered that as she alighted, ignoring the helping hand Dan offered. "He'll be along directly. He's walking."

"Walkin'?" the hostler stuttered. "*Him*—walkin'?"

"My luggage, please," she said. "I'll need a cab to the hotel if there's one to be had."

Dan spoke to the openmouthed hostler. "What's going on? Why are all those people bunched down there?"

"It's the trial," the man mumbled, still staring unbelievingly from Dan to the girl. "The jury's about to come in."

"Jury?"

"It's the murder trial," the man answered. "Didn't you know that Bart Webb has finally been called to account fer killin' Ed Vickers?"

Dan felt the blood rush out of his face. "What?" he exclaimed. "Ed Vickers killed! Good God!"

He started striding toward the plaza. Someone in the gathering lifted a shout: "They're comin' in! They've reached a verdict!"

The throng surged up the wide stone steps into the courthouse door, but there were so many they backed up like floodwaters, and the majority were forced to remain outside.

Dan discovered that Jennifer Spring was hurrying along at his heels. He glanced back at her and was surprised to see how agitated she seemed.

He sensed that the crowd ahead was in an ugly mood. His hand went instinctively to his side, as though to reassure himself of something. But his gun was not there. Along with his other possessions it was packed in his small traveling case in the boot of the stagecoach. He had not carried a side gun since that evening in Wagonbox.

As he reached the fringe of the crowd he saw that not

everyone had joined in the surge to be the first to hear the jury's verdict. Two men stood apart, backed up against the monument to veterans of the Indian Wars. They were cowhands, seamy and well up in years. They were silent and grim, dressed in their best white cotton shirts and Saturday-night pants, with worn old boots shined. One was a black man. He was weaponless, but his companion, a grizzled, bowlegged waddie, had a heavy cap-and-ball Colt slung in a time-scarred holster. They stood there together like men who might be called on to die, and were ready.

A spreading silence came from the court building, flowed out of the wide entrance, down the crowded steps and to the plaza. "They're readin' it," someone whispered.

Dan could hear the breathing of men nearby. Some were miners by their garb, others wore the checked shirts and stovepipe boots of freighters. There were bearded sheepmen and a rich sprinkling of ranch hands and well-dressed owners.

A voice sounded. "Not guilty! *Not* guilty!" The speaker sounded stunned, incredulous. He could see that his listeners did not believe they had heard correctly. "*Not* guilty!" he repeated. "They're turnin' Bart Webb loose ag'in."

"Them cowards!" a man screeched. "Them yaller jurors! They was afeared to do their duty. We ought to lynch 'em!"

Dan saw that the speaker was Pete Slater, the rock-jawed man who had just arrived on the stagecoach with Abel Jenkins.

Jenkins himself was in the crowd and now spoke. "Don't blame the jurors! They know what would happen to them or their wives an' kids. The same thing that's been happenin' to them poor devils down in the basin. It ain't them that ought to be strung up. It's Bart Webb!"

"Git a rope!" Pete Slater yelled. "We ain't goin' to let that devil stay alive, air we? Git—"

His voice faded off. The two ancient cowboys had moved. Arm in arm they came slicing through the crowd, parting it as

9

a ship's prow parts water. The grizzled one had not drawn his gun, but there was that look on his face that meant business.

They surged to the steps of the courthouse, mounted it, and stood, backs to the open door. The doorway and the steps around them suddenly cleared, leaving them there alone. No word had been spoken by them, no threats made. Outnumbered forty to one, they dominated the plaza. Dead silence fell.

Two persons emerged from the courthouse. One was lean and gray as a timber wolf, grained by weather and time. He wore a white cotton shirt and a black string tie and well-fitted, checked saddle pants, cuffed high over half boots. His garb was neat, but a trifle threadbare, his boots gleaming, but obviously far past their prime.

With him was a handsome woman of about his own age. She had Mexican eyes, Mexican velvet skin, the carriage of pride and breeding. A small lace mantilla partly covered her hair, which was tinged with gray. She held to her husband's arm. In her fine features was no fear, only scorn for those she faced. She wore a wide-skirted dress in the Spanish fashion, but it was obviously a heritage from the past, brought out for this occasion.

The two time-worn cowhands moved to the sides of the couple.

Then a woman in the crowd screamed, "No! No, Lennie!"

A lanky youth, who appeared to be about fifteen, had stepped into the path of the quartet, blocking their way.

Again the woman screamed the appeal. "Lennie! No! Please! No!"

She moved into the cleared space that had opened magically. It had been some five years since Dan had seen Tansie Vickers. She was still flashingly handsome, yellow-haired, and bold enough to use powder along with a touch of rouge and eyelash blackening. She had been the belle of a trail-town dance hall in the Wyoming settlement where Dan had been town marshal when she had been married to Ed Vickers. Dan had been Ed Vickers' best man at the ceremony.

Tansie Vickers was frightened now, her lips a pale smear against the pallor of her face. The youth who was facing the quartet had a six-shooter in his hand, and it was cocked. The weapon looked awkwardly cumbersome in his grasp, for he was so young none of his clothes and boots seemed to exactly fit. Lennie Vickers had been only nine when Dan had last seen him, and he was now growing into a maturing image of his brother. And, like his brother, he was brave, unafraid of odds.

"No you don't, Mr. Webb," he said to the gray-haired man, his voice shrill with strain. "You ain't just walkin' away free an' laughin' while my brother lies in the grave where you put him. Go fer your gun. I'm goin' to shoot you!"

Bart Webb and his wife halted. "I'm not armed, Lennie," Bart Webb said.

Lennie Vickers' knees were trembling. So was his voice. He spoke to Bart Webb's cowboys. "Give him a gun, one of you."

"I didn't kill your brother, Lennie," Bart Webb said. "I never shot at a man in my life unless he was facin' me."

Abel Jenkins moved from among the onlookers and offered Bart Webb a six-shooter. Webb impatiently pushed the gun aside. "Stay out of this, Jenkins," he said.

"Take it, Mr. Webb," Lennie Vickers said, his voice running up the scale. "Don't make me shoot you down this way."

"Go ahead an' shoot, Lennie," Abel Jenkins snarled. "You got every right."

Dan saw the look in young Lennie Vickers' eyes. Lennie had gone too far to back down. He meant to shoot Bart Webb.

Dan moved in, covering the distance in long strides. He came up back of the youth and grasped the six-shooter, jamming the hammer with his fingers. He discovered that Bart Webb's wife had moved in front of her husband, willing to take the bullet in order to save him. Dan's mind flashed back to another day, to another wife who had made that sacrifice.

11

He whirled Lennie around, holding him a prisoner. "Take it easy, fella," he said, pushing the pistol down so that its muzzle faced the ground.

Tansie Vickers came rushing in and threw her arms around Lennie, pushing Dan aside. She faced Bart Webb. "You'd even kill a boy!" she choked. "You and these night riders you've hired to terrorize us."

"My God, Mrs. Vickers!" Bart Webb protested wildly. "I never killed your husband. The jury exonerated me. I was miles away that night."

"Of course!" Tansie sobbed. "You're always miles away. Well, you've won, I don't want Lennie murdered too. I'll quit. I'll get out of Eagle Basin. That's what you want, isn't it?"

Bart Webb made a gesture of futility and turned, walking away with his wife clinging to his arm. His two riders followed close at their heels.

Tansie Vickers began to sway. Dan steadied her and she quickly strengthened. "Oh, Dan, Dan!" she sobbed. "How did you get here? Where did you come from after all these years?"

She placed her arms around his neck and kissed him, clinging to him and weeping.

"Lennie sent for me," Dan said.

"Lennie?" she exclaimed. She turned on the youth and it seemed to Dan there was sudden anger in her—and fear. "You never told me, young man. You shouldn't have done it, Lennie. You'll only make things worse. It isn't fair to Dan. He'll only be—be killed too."

Lennie Vickers was staring worshipfully at Dan. "It really is you, ain't it?" he choked. "You never answered my letter an' I had give up on you comin' to help us."

"I just got off the stage," Dan said. "Your letter lay for a month in the post office at Wagonbox. I was drifting around Wyoming, hunting, fishing, and wasn't picking up my mail. I came as fast as I could."

12

He paused and added slowly, "Looks like I got here too late. When did it happen? Ed's death?"

"Two weeks ago," Tansie said. "Let's go somewhere so we can tell you all about it. We're staying at the Stockade Hotel. It's just down the street. There's so much to tell, so terribly much."

She linked arms with Dan and began pushing through the bystanders. Dan discovered that one of these was Jennifer Spring. She still wore the ankle-length coat, with dust in the creases, as well as the concealing veil. "Well, well!" she said. "You're not as spineless as you put on. Or don't you know you might have been killed trying to grab a cocked pistol from a scared boy?"

"I'd say I was closer to cashing in my chips when I thought of riding in a stagecoach with a certain lady driver on the box," Dan said, grinning.

She smiled, and was turning away when another figure loomed up. This was a burly, bulldog-jawed man who had the star of a sheriff pinned to his vest. A quid of tobacco lumped his cheek. He wore a gun.

He blocked Dan's path. "'Scuse me, Mrs. Vickers," he said to Tansie, touching the brim of his hat. "I want to make sure you know what you're doin'. Do you know this man?"

"Of course I do," Tansie said.

"You mean you really know that he's Dan Cameron," the sheriff said unbelievingly.

"I do," she said. "He's an old friend of mine and of my poor husband. Dan, this is Sheriff Jim Honeywell."

"Howdy," Dan said, extending a hand.

Honeywell ignored the hand. "Ain't things rough enough around here without you showin' up, Cameron?" he said plaintively. "We don't want no more gunfighters to deal with."

"Gunfighters?" Dan's tone caused Honeywell to take a hasty step back and set himself for trouble.

"No offense, no offense," Honeywell protested. "It's jest

thet some citizens don't seem to think the law can protect 'em any longer an' are importin' fellers like you."

"You're a fool, Jim Honeywell!" Tansie said. "Dan Cameron's not that kind any more than was my husband, even though people tried to put that brand on them. Dan and Ed were peace officers in tough towns along the cattle trails and they brought law and order. That's more than you've done in this county. My husband came here to homestead, to live in peace and forget the bad old days. Now he's dead. Now his brother's life isn't safe, even if he's hardly more than a boy. Nor is my life safe. What few of us are left in Eagle Basin live in fear, and you do nothing."

"Thet ain't fair, Mrs. Vickers," Honeywell protested. "I only got one deputy in a county that stretches all the way to the border. What kin only two of us do ag'in—"

He broke it off abruptly, but Tansie finished it for him. "Against Bart Webb," she said. "You're afraid of him, Jim. Admit it."

"I didn't mention no names, an' I ain't afeared of Bart Webb, nor any man alive," Jim Honeywell said grimly.

Tansie again took Dan's arm to lead him and Lennie toward the hotel. And Dan, once more, found Jennifer Spring in his path. She had been listening. "You *are* just full of surprises, Mr. Cameron," she said. "I never dreamed my stage companion was the notorious Dan Cameron."

"Who are you?" Tansie demanded.

"Just a visitor in town," Jennifer Spring said, and walked away, also heading for the hotel.

CHAPTER TWO

Jennifer Spring was signing the register at the desk when Dan and Tansie entered, followed by Lennie. Tansie and Lennie got their keys and they mounted to the second floor. Tansie ushered them into her room, which was equipped with the customary meager, plain furnishings. She motioned Dan to a chair, but kept pacing the room nervously. Lennie sat on the edge of the bed.

"Ed wrote to you," she said. "It was after—after we heard about Madge. Even then it was weeks after it had happened. Ed happened to be going through the old newspapers here at the Stockade when we were here to do some buying. He wrote to you at once. But you didn't answer."

"I'm sorry," Dan said. "I finally got the letter, but I just couldn't answer. I didn't want to talk about it, even in a letter. I was sort of at loose ends. Just roaming around. I quit wearing the badge right after it happened."

"I understand," she said. "It was a terrible thing. On your wedding day. How awful."

That brought it all maddeningly back in Dan's mind. Coming out of the little church in the rowdy boom town, where the saloons outnumbered the single church thirty to one, with his bride on his arm—the gentle Madge Williams, who had fallen in love with the tall young marshal who was rated as one of the deadliest men with a gun among the peace officers along the cattle trails.

They had been deliriously happy at that moment. The waiting carriage had been adorned with cowbells, tinware, and just-married banners and in it they were to ride away into the clouds on their honeymoon.

Then the gunshot. Only Madge Williams had sensed what was coming in time, and had stepped in front of Dan. The assassin was also dead in the next instant, paying with his life for nursing a grudge over some minor affront that had festered in his mind. Dan, with his left arm supporting his bride, had snatched a pistol from the holster of a bystander and had fired the return shot so swiftly that the two concussions stirred the small bell in the church tower to sound one sad note of mourning.

Madge Williams tried to smile up at him. She had whispered, "I love you!" She had still clutched her bridal bouquet. The flowers had been red with the end of their bliss. Then she was gone.

"It was hard on both me an' Ed," Tansie was saying. "We were so far away and it was too late to try to come to Wagonbox. Madge was a very close friend."

Dan decided that Tansie was letting time blur her memories. As a dance-hall girl she had lived in a different world from the girl who had died in his arms. Madge Williams had been the daughter of a Texas cattleman who had trailed herds into Wyoming and finally had made his home there.

Tansie waited for Dan to speak, but he remained silent, living again with the phantoms and the regrets. She studied him from beneath her penciled eyebrows. She had put on weight, which she was trying to conceal with corseting. "I didn't know that Lennie had sent a letter to you, Dan," she said. "What did he say?"

The bluntness of the question somewhat nettled Dan. He had always liked Tansie for her breezy, good-natured ways, but he had never really expected the marriage to last when she and Ed had left Wyoming for faraway Eagle Basin to become sodbusters and start life anew.

Lennie himself answered her question. "I told Dan that Ed an' me was havin' trouble with a range hog down here," he

16

said bluntly. "But I wrote too late. Bart Webb murdered my brother from ambush while my letter set waitin' in that Wyomin' post office. Bart Webb is out to drive all us homesteaders out of the basin so he kin build up his Circle W spread."

"You shouldn't have come here, Dan," Tansie said. "Go back to Wyoming. Lennie should never have written to you. He did that without my permission. There's nothing here for you—except to be murdered if you interfere."

"Interfere?" Dan asked. "In what?"

She decided not to answer that. Dan took her arm, seated her in the only rocking chair in the room. "Tell me all about it," he urged. "Why was Ed killed? When did all this start?"

"Months ago," she said, fighting to control her voice. "Without warning, without reason. Bart Webb must have gone insane. We had been doing well. Ed and Lennie were clearing more land for crops, finding enough work on the side to keep us going. Ed even made some money breaking horses for Bart Webb at the Circle W. Then it started. Night riders began shooting up the homes of settlers. Two settlers were murdered in those raids. People, in terror, began leaving. There are only three or four settlers left in addition to our place, and some of those are back in the draws almost out of the basin. We were raided. Shots were fired into the house at night several times. Finally it happened. Ed was murdered."

"Shot in the back by Bart Webb," Lennie spoke, his voice bitter.

"The jury didn't seem to think so, Lennie," Dan said gently.

"The jury was afeared to convict him," Lennie said. "Ed had gone out after dark to look after the horses what were millin' around in the pasture beyond the crick that runs through the claim. He thought it might be a cougar. We heard a shot. When he didn't come back I went lookin' an' found him dead. When daybreak come I found the tracks of Bart Webb's horse."

17

"How do you know it was Webb's horse?"

"It was that big Morgan ropin' horse that he rides. It's the biggest saddlehorse I ever seen, and it's in a class by itself as a cuttin' horse on roundup or at calf brand. Bart Webb won't let any other man ride it. He's mighty particular about keepin' it shod sharp and clean. Old Mose Lee, what has worked for the Circle W since he was a slave, does the blacksmithin' over there."

"Someone else could have been riding that horse without his knowledge," Dan said.

"Not old Sultan. He won't stand fer anyone but Bart Webb on his back, an' he's mean when he objects. It was Bart Webb. His wife an' some of his cowhands testified that he was asleep at the ranch the night Ed was murdered. They lied."

"Is this the first time he's been arrested?" Dan asked.

"He's been suspected before, but never actually went to trial," Tansie answered.

"He always seems to have—what is it you call it?—an alibi," Lennie said. "Just like this time."

"Whatever evidence did they have against him outside of the horseshoe tracks?" Dan asked.

"Well, everybody knows he's a killer."

"How do they know that?" Dan asked.

"Fer one thing he was a sharpshooter in the War Between the States," Lennie said. "Fought on the side o' the South. Most folks around here was Union men. They say Bart Webb must have killed a lot of men when he was in the war."

Dan winced. Here it was again—the killer brand.

Lennie saw his expression and guessed its source. He gulped. "I didn't mean anythin' like that about you, Dan," he said hastily. "I know you was a lawman in some rough towns. So was Ed. But Bart Webb is different. He's got no heart, no soul. He's made of steel."

Dan felt cold inside. These same things had been said about himself in the past.

"Dan, what are your plans?" Tansie asked.

Dan shrugged. "Where does the wind blow? And what about you? Are you really going to leave this country?"

"Yes," she said. "I have relatives in Nebraska. They are farmers like Ed wanted to be. I'll have to depend on them until I can find something to do. Lennie will go with me."

Dan feared that he knew what that meant. Back to the dance halls for Tansie Vickers, who had been born Anastasia Swinberg, child of honest, God-fearing Minnesota parents.

"I'm stayin' here," Lennie spoke grimly.

"We'll talk it over tomorrow," Dan said. "I'll see if I can get a room here for the night."

"There's nothin' to talk over," Lennie said. "I ain't lettin' that murderer rob us of our home. Me an' Ed worked hard to build a house an' clear land. Ed sweat in a sawpit up at the mines cuttin' timber fer the stopes to earn money. We both chopped cotton down in the hot valley in summer. We hunted an' trapped coyotes fer the sheepmen in winter."

"And hunted for the treasure," Tansie said tartly. "At least Ed wasted a lot of time down at that old mission tryin' to git rich overnight instead of sweatin' in a sawpit or choppin' cotton."

"Treasure?" Dan asked.

"It's another of those fool stories like you hear everywhere in this country," Tansie said. "Instead of a lost gold mine this one is about a bunch of pirates from China or some such place, whose ship was wrecked on the California Coast, and who was wiped out by Indians after they sacked Santa Rosalia."

"Santa Rosalia?"

"That's the name of the mission in the basin. It was abandoned years ago an' has been almost turned into a pile of adobe by people like Ed who thought the treasure might have been buried there."

"There ain't any treasure," Lennie sniffed. "It's nothin' but a bunch of lies."

"That's generally the case," Dan said. He arose and headed for the door. "I'll see you later."

He descended to the clerk's desk. Dusk had settled and lamps were burning in the small sitting room off the desk. Beyond was a dining room where waitresses were busy placing silver and linen on tables.

Outside, the street was quiet. A few wagons and buggies still creaked by, last of the citizens of the county who had come to Rimrock to see Bart Webb convicted of murder, now on their way homeward. Several guests were checking out of the hotel. The Roman holiday was over.

"I need a room for the night," Dan told the clerk.

The clerk, a fleshless man with a hooked nose and a color-less, drooping mustache, started to spin the ledger around so that Dan could sign. Then he took a second look at Dan. He hastily closed the ledger.

"All filled up," he said. "Sorry, mister."

Dan gazed at him. "You're not good at lying," he said. "This bat's nest is half empty." He reached out, opened the ledger, and glanced at the rack in back of the table on which the room keys hung, each under a number.

"Number 15 has always been a lucky number for me at roulette," he said. He moved back of the desk, took the key from its hook. He signed the ledger.

"Daniel Cameron is the name," he said. "You seem to have heard of it. How much?"

"One dollar," the man croaked. "Don't blame me, Mr. Cameron. It's jest that we don't want no trouble here at the Stockade."

"With Bart Webb, you mean?" Dan asked. "Did you get your orders from him?"

"I didn't git my orders from nobody," the man stammered. "It's jest that I heard—I heard—"

"That you heard of Dan Cameron and his rep as a killer," Dan said. "I'll try not to do any bloodletting while I'm a guest here, my friend. I'll pay my bill when I leave."

He pocketed the key, left the hotel, and walked down the street to the stage station where he found his luggage in the dingy waiting room. It consisted of a suitcase and a leather carrier.

As he was leaving the office with his burden a burly man alighted from an empty ore wagon which had just pulled into town. He was Clem Coates, the stage driver who had been left afoot down the trail by the audacious Jennifer Spring.

Clem Coates was in an ugly mood. He recognized Dan and jabbed a finger against his chest, halting him. "You was one of them thet saw that cussed female push me down in a gully an' let her drive away, leavin' me marooned," he snarled. "I walked two miles afore a freighter came along an' picked me up."

"Get that finger off me," Dan said, "before you lose it."

Instead, Clem Coates pushed harder. "Who was that female?" he demanded. "Whar is she?"

Dan moved aside, and Coates, off balance, staggered forward. He recovered and whirled, cursing Dan. He came in, a fist swinging. Dan blocked the blow, swung a left to a point just below the rib cage. He dropped his luggage and finished the bigger man with a right to the jaw. Coates staggered sickly back, then sagged to hands and knees, retching and slobbering.

Dan placed a boot against the man's rear and shoved. Coates pitched flat on his face. "Next time," Dan said, "mind your manners."

Clem Coates rolled over, trying to get to his feet. He began clawing at a six-shooter which was thrust into his leather belt. Dan moved in, stepped on his arm, pinning it down, and yanked the gun from Coates's belt. He flipped open the cylinder, shook out the shells, and hurled them away. He tossed the gun out of reach.

Coates got groggily to his knees. "'Twon't do you no good!" he raged. "I'll be comin' at you till I git you."

The hostler spoke. "Take it easy, Clem. Don't go talkin' out o' turn. You might be takin' on more'n you kin handle."

"What?" Coates gritted. "As soon as I git my gun I'll kill him."

"He ain't armed, Clem," the hostler said. "Lucky fer you, maybe."

"Lucky fer me?" Coates snarled. "What kind o' talk is that. You know I could handle him an'—"

"I reckon you don't know who he is, Clem," the hostler said. "His name is Cameron—Dan Cameron—from Wyomin'."

"What in blazes do I keer who he is an'—" Clem Coates began. Then a light dawned. "Oh!" he said, his voice trailing off weakly. He said nothing more, merely sitting there, nursing an aching jaw with a big, hairy hand.

Dan shouldered his luggage and turned to walk away. "I couldn't have done better myself," a feminine voice said.

Again it was the girl from the stagecoach, Jennifer Spring. She was sitting in a dilapidated hansom cab that had just pulled up at the curb. A toothy, gray-haired black man, who wore a coachman's ancient hat and jacket, alighted and opened the door to permit her to step to the sidewalk.

"We're here on the same errand, I see," she said, stepping over the outstretched legs of the dazed Clem Coates. "I came for my belongings. I'm stopping at the Stockade Hotel too, and would be glad to share the cab if you don't mind waiting a moment."

Dan tossed his luggage into the vehicle and made an elaborate bow. "It will be a pleasure," he said, "as long as you are not doing the driving, my lady."

"For that remark I should leave you afoot," she said.

The hostler and cab driver brought out a trunk, which they placed on the rack on top of the vehicle. They added a considerable collection of smaller luggage and hatboxes to the load.

Dan eyed the assembly. "Seems like you aim to stay awhile," he observed.

She offered a hand, by which he ushered her ceremoniously into the cab. He crowded in beside her among the overflow of luggage. Clem Coates was still sitting on the sidewalk, staring incredulously.

"I've taken a liking to this country," she said. "It could be that I might become a permanent resident."

"Under what name?" Dan asked.

He felt that she was looking down her nose at him from beneath the veil. "As far as you are concerned," she said, "my name is Jennifer Spring. Hasn't it ever occurred to you, Mr. Man from Wyoming, that it isn't polite to question the right of a lady to go by any name she pleases, not to mention engaging in fist brawls in public streets?"

"I'll remember," Dan said.

"Here's the hotel," she said, as the cab lurched to a stop. "It's nice talking to you, Mr. Cameron. I hope the climate agrees with you. Goodbye."

"Adiós," Dan said, alighting and helping her out. "That's Spanish, for hoping I'll talk to you again."

"It's Spanish for goodbye," she said sweetly. "Goodbye."

A hotel flunky carried her luggage. Dan shouldered his own belongings and followed them to the second floor, where she entered a room at the front while he found his way to his own quarters a distance toward the rear.

He got out fresh socks, shirt, and underwear, descended to the lobby, and asked directions to a barbershop. There he was shaved and permitted to sluice off the dust of the trip in a tin tub, with soap and towel thrown in, all for a total of thirty cents.

Darkness had come when he returned to the hotel. He went to his room to replenish his cigar case, and when he unlocked the door he discovered that a small white envelope had been thrust over the threshold during his absence. It was sealed and carried only his penned name.

Tearing it open he found a plain sheet of writing paper bearing a message. A fragment of gold and green paper fluttered to the floor. He picked it up. It was the torn half of a hundred-dollar banknote.

He stared unbelievingly at it, then read the message:

The other half is yours. I want to talk to you privately. Be at my office at nine tonight.

Willis Mason

Frowning, Dan read the words again. He finally thrust the paper and the portion of banknote in his pocket. He stood debating with himself for a time. Then, slowly, and at times deciding against it, he finally delved to the bottom of his suitcase, and drew out a holstered six-shooter and belt. The pistol was a .44 Colt, blue-muzzled, with a black handle, finely balanced. He had carried it in wild trail towns when he had been fair game for lawless and reckless men who had sought fame by trying to outbluff or outdraw the noted town-tamer, Dan Cameron.

This gun had killed, and it had brought on the grudge that had cost the life of his bride. He had packed it away the same day Madge had died in his arms, vowing never to wear it again. All he had wanted was to forget. Now the weapon had the reassuring touch of an old friend, the promise of unfailing loyalty.

He made sure it was clean and loaded with five live shells and the customary empty under the hammer. He adjusted the belt around his waist, nudging it into its old familiar position under his hand on his thigh. He left the room, locking the door, then tapped on the door of Tansie's room.

"Ready?" he called. Both Tansie and Lennie were in the room, ready and waiting. They instantly took notice of the gun at his side.

"You shouldn't!" Tansie exclaimed.

Lennie said, "Good gosh!" His eyes were wide, delighted.

It was as though he had suddenly found a strong arm on his shoulder.

They descended the stairs, walked through the sitting room into the dining room, which sported linen and silverware on the table.

"Just like the Harvey Houses on the Santa Fe," Dan said.

"They try to be civilized," Tansie said. "At least here. It's different in the basin."

Dan ordered steaks, which he and Lennie enjoyed, but Tansie only dabbled at her food. She was pale, nervous.

Dan studied Lennie. The soberness of prematurity was tightening his mouth, further thinning his features so that his cheekbones were gaunt, almost like Dan's own.

"I'm anxious to see this Eagle Basin," Dan said.

"You're goin' there?" Lennie exclaimed, a rising delight in his voice.

"Of course," Dan said. "With you and Tansie."

Tansie spoke dully. "You mean you're not going back to Wyoming, Dan?"

"Not now at least," Dan said. "There's no hurry."

"But there is!" she burst out.

"Why? What do you mean?" he asked.

"I—I don't know what I mean," she chattered. "I guess I'm too upset to think straight."

"Who is Willis Mason?" Dan asked after a time, trying to be casual.

Tansie seemed startled. "Willis Mason? Now, why do you ask about him? Do you know him?"

"No," Dan said. "Tell me about him."

It was Lennie who answered. His voice was bitter. "He's Bart Webb's friend," he said. "He's a lawyer an' a politician. He's a bigwig down at the state capital, an' they say he's goin' to be appointed territorial governor one of these days. At least he's tryin' to git the job. He's got an office here in Rimrock, for he's got his finger in county politics, but he's from the basin. He's got a big home in Pinedale where he lives when he ain't here or at the capital. He's got servants. Never got married."

"Did you say he was Bart Webb's friend?" Dan asked.

"Willis Mason stands up for that coyote," Lennie said. "He claims folks are wrong about Bart Webb."

"Where is his office here in Rimrock?" Dan asked.

Lennie suddenly drew into himself, suspicion dawning in his freckled face. "It's down the street past the courthouse in the Mason buildin'," he said distantly. "He owns the buildin' an' rents some of it to other lawyers an' such. You won't have no trouble findin' it."

The meal was finished in strained silence. Lennie had suddenly become grim and hostile. Tansie ate nothing more. Her fingers trembled as she tried to drink the coffee that was served with the pie. She was visibly anxious to get the meal over with, and hurried the pace as they left the dining room.

"Good night!" she said, moving ahead alone and heading for the stairs. "I'm tired and want to turn in."

Dan looked at his watch. The hour was still short of eight o'clock. "How about a game of pool?" he said to Lennie.

"No, thanks," Lennie answered curtly. "I've got other things to do."

He turned to leave, but Dan halted him. "Tell me about it, Lennie," he said gently. "I know that you came out here to live with Ed and Tansie after your folks died in Nebraska three or four years ago. I met you that time your folks came to Wyoming to visit your brother. You were only about nine then. Now you're a man. What I want to know is what's going on. Why are you so bitter against Willis Mason?"

"I jest told you," Lennie said. "He's on Bart Webb's side."

"And what is Webb after?"

"Land," Lennie said. "More range fer cattle. What else? He's got a run-down outfit in the east end of the basin called the Circle W. He used to run cattle all over the basin, but when the government opened it to homesteadin' some years

26

ago it about ruined him. So he's set out to git all the basin back by scarin' the settlers out."

"When did all this start?"

"You mean the killin' an' the night ridin'? It's been goin' on fer months. Maybe nigh onto a year."

"Only for months?" Dan asked. "But the basin was opened to homesteading some years ago. It was five years ago when Ed and Tansie came here to take up a claim. Why did Bart Webb wait so long to begin pushing people around?"

"Why don't you ask him?" Lennie snapped. "Or Willis Mason? Or Max Largo?"

"Max Largo? He's here?"

"You do know him, then," Lennie said caustically. "I figgered so. Like you know Willis Mason. Largo packs a gun too —like you."

"I've never laid eyes on Willis Mason in my life, to my knowledge," Dan said slowly. "I've got reasons for asking about him. But Max Largo's a shingle off another tree. Yes, I know him, and nothing good. He's a gunslinger. Fast, dangerous. He'll kill for money. I deadlined him out of Wagonbox up in Wyoming a time back. You mean he's here in Rimrock?"

"Looks like he ain't the only gunslinger thet's bein' brought in by Willis Mason," Lennie said. He walked away, heading out of the hotel and vanished along the sidewalk.

Dan suddenly turned, mounted the stairs to the rooms above, and tapped on the door of Tansie's quarters. "It's Dan," he said. "I want to talk to you, Tansie."

"I'm too tired to talk," she answered. "I just don't feel like—"

The roar of a gunshot from outside the hotel brought a scream from her. Dan heard shattered glass falling in the room. "Tansie!" he shouted.

When there was no answer, he twisted the doorknob. The door was locked. He backed away, charged and tore the cheap lock from its fastenings, and burst into the room.

27

"Tansie!" She was crouched alongside the bed, ashen, sobbing hysterically. She had been preparing for bed.

The lower sash of one of the two windows had been raised for ventilation. A bullet had smashed through both panes of glass. The wick in the oil lamp in a bracket on the wall still flickered in gusts of air.

"Are you hurt?" Dan asked. Tansie was unable to speak, frozen by terror. But she had not been hit. The bullet had torn into the ceiling after shattering the windowpanes and could not possibly have struck her.

CHAPTER THREE

Dan raced to the open window, crouching and peering over the sill. The window was at the front corner of the hotel and overlooked a considerable portion of Rimrock's principal street. Men were emerging from the doors of saloons and eating houses and peering around, seeking the source of the gunshot and the shattered glass. Voices were rising, asking questions.

Directly across the street were several flat-roofed, single-story buildings, the majority with false fronts. Dan felt that the shot must have come from the roof of one of those structures, but the false fronts would have covered the escape of the person who had fired. The brisk breeze would have dissipated powder smoke by this time.

One of the buildings housed a billiard parlor, and men were emerging from its door to stand on the sidewalk, peering around. One was Bart Webb. With him were the two seamy-faced riders Dan had seen at the courthouse. Bart Webb had a pool cue in his hand.

"What happened?" Webb asked.

"Looks like somebody shot out a window in the Stockade," someone answered.

Seeeing Dan's head at the window, Webb lifted his voice. "Anybody hurt up there?"

"Nobody hurt," Dan answered. He added, "Not yet."

Bart Webb stood for a space as though considering the meaning of that last remark. Then, as though washing his hands of the affair, he turned and walked back into the billiard parlor, followed by his riders.

The hotel clerk had arrived at the door. There were other inquisitive faces at his shoulder.

"There are two busted windowpanes and a bullet in the ceiling," Dan said. "There seems to be someone who took a shot at Mrs. Vickers' room."

"Likely some drunk letting off steam," the man said. "I'm George Smythe, and I own this hotel. It's time Jim Honeywell put a stop to things like this. We'll move Mrs. Vickers to another room right away. That's all, folks. Just a drunk. Nobody hurt."

Dan felt that George Smythe was a little too anxious to write off the incident. He was on the point of asking questions, but decided against it. He felt that all he would get was evasion.

Lennie arrived, pushing past George Smythe into the room. He eyed the damage and spoke to Tansie. "What happened?"

She was still trembling and unable to answer. Dan spoke for her. "Somebody shot out the glass in the window."

"Where was you when it happened?" Lennie asked pointedly.

Dan ignored that. "Make sure Mrs. Vickers' room has a good lock and that there are curtains and blinds on the windows. It might be better if she was moved into a room next to Lennie's. She might feel better if she knew her brother-in-law was near."

Lennie opened his mouth to object, then closed his lips and accepted the situation.

As the change was being made Sheriff Jim Honeywell arrived belatedly, and spent time asking futile questions. He seemed glad to accept George Smythe's opinion that it had been the aimless work of a drunken man wanting to create excitement. He finally barged away, saying he would look around for the culprit.

Dan waited until all of them had left. "You'll be all right

now, Tansie," he said. "You know that shot wasn't really intended to hit you, don't you?"

She did not answer. She was still terrified. Dan turned to leave the room.

"Where you goin', Mr. Cameron?" Lennie asked harshly.

"To see a man," Dan said.

"Willis Mason, maybe," Lennie said. "What's the pay fer gunmen nowdays?"

"It comes pretty high at times," Dan said. "What's a man's life worth?"

He left then. His first objective was the billiard parlor across the street. Bart Webb had quit playing pool and he and his two companions were sitting in chairs along the wall, sipping from bottles of beer. Except for the proprietor, a beefy, balding man in a striped silk shirt who stood in back of the small counter, there were no others in the long room.

The fact that the black cowboy was drinking with his companions was proof of the fear in which Bart Webb was held, for there was a faded sign on the wall stating that Indians and Negroes would not be served in this place.

The black man had once been mighty of strength by the spread of his shoulders and looked as if he could still take good care of himself in a fight. The white old-timer had been burned almost as dark as his companion by wind and weather and sun. He was smaller, warped of leg, with a nose that almost met his chin. His hands were gnarled, rope-worn.

Neither Bart Webb nor his two men was armed. At least there were no weapons in sight.

Dan looked at Webb. "I'm a stranger in these parts," he said. "I've decided I might get me a piece of land and hang around for a while."

"Why tell me?" Bart Webb answered.

"Where could I find some good land, easy to plant, with water and comfort? Land that nobody else wants."

Bart Webb remained cool, gray. "It's a free country," he

said. "The federal land office is at the courthouse. You should inquire there tomorrow. They have maps, Cameron."

"You seem to know me," Dan said.

"By reputation," Bart Webb said.

The small, wizened cowboy came to his feet like a game-cock. "If it's trouble yo're lookin' fer, mister, you come to the right place. Put up yore dukes an'—"

"Back off, Bandy," Bart Webb said. "I'll handle this."

The gamecock reluctantly resumed his seat, squirted tobacco juice into a cuspidor, and glared belligerently at Dan.

"Anything else we can do for you?" Bart Webb asked.

"Someone shot out the window in Mrs. Vickers' room, as you know," Dan said. "If you happen to find out who did it, let me know. I want him to pay for the damage."

"What makes you think I might find out?" Bart Webb asked.

"I figured the shot was fired from the roof of one of these buildings," Dan said. "Maybe from this one."

He turned and walked out of the room. He carried with him puzzlement and a deep sense of frustration. And annoyance. He had not intended to throw down the gauntlet to the rancher by declaring himself in line for a homestead. He had surprised himself by the announcement. It was as though he was recanting on his vow to never again be involved in violence. Now he was taking up the cause of Tansie Vickers and of her husband who had been murdered from ambush.

Dan and Ed Vickers had been fast friends. They had been comrades in arms in the rough world of booming frontier towns. They had formed a team, both young, both a trifle arrogant, no doubt, because of their abilities and of their reputations as hard men. There had been no jealousy between them, only an iron bond that had been forged in the common possibility of sudden death. Dan had owed his life to Ed Vickers more than once, just as Ed had owed his life to Dan when they had stood shoulder to shoulder against odds—and had won.

He had these thoughts to burden him as he walked down the street, passed the plaza, and found the building Lennie had mentioned. It was an oblong two-story structure, freshly painted in white with cream trim, and had Willis Mason's name chiseled in the stone arch across the entrance. Rented offices opened down the length of a dimly lit corridor. A clothing store occupied the front street corner. A directory on the wall in the corridor told that Willis Mason's office was on the second floor. He mounted the stairs and tapped on the door whose frosted glass bore the name:

WILLIS MASON
ATTORNEY AT LAW

A key turned in the lock, the door opened, and Dan found himself facing Max Largo, the gunman with whom he had clashed in the days that he hoped were past.

"Come in, Cameron," Largo said. He was a lean, olive-skinned man with pale gravestone eyes in a face whose swart skin seemed a trifle small for the bony, sharp-jawed structure of his face. He was in shirtsleeves, wearing a white cotton shirt tucked into dark, belted pants. He wore a holstered six-shooter.

"Yes, Cameron," another voice spoke. "Come in! Come in! Welcome!"

The speaker arose from a leather swivel chair at a flat-topped desk which had papers stacked in neat piles. "I'm Willis Mason," he said, extending a hand.

Dan briefly shook hands. Willis Mason offered an opened box of cigars and motioned him toward a chair. Decanters of liquors stood on a wheeled serving table nearby. The office was richly carpeted. Money had been spent on oil paintings and wallpaper.

Dan refused both the cigars and the liquor. Willis Mason was a man of perhaps sixty, he judged, with bushy, graying hair, a clipped gray mustache, and wore a tailored dark business suit. He had wide shoulders, fleshy jowls, and strong teeth, which were often visible. His voice carried the ring and resonance of an orator.

"You and Max seem to be acquainted," Mason said as he helped himself to one of the cigars, and used a gold clipper to sever its tip.

"We've met," Dan said.

Mason laughed. "So I understand," he said. "Well, we must let bygones be bygones. Max, I don't need you any longer."

He lighted his cigar and waited until the gunman had left and the door had been closed. He tipped back in his chair and surveyed Dan from head to foot.

"You measure up to things I've heard about you, Cameron," he said.

"Such as?" Dan asked.

Mason waved that aside. "I hear that some wild woman aboard your coach today marooned Clem Coates, and you had to drive the rig into town, leaving Clem afoot," he said, chuckling. "She must be one of these female Amazons they talk about these days."

"It was quite a trip," Dan said.

"They tell me her name is Jennifer Spring," Mason said. "At least that's the name she gave when she bought passage on the coach. Are you acquainted with this lady?"

"I never laid eyes on her before today," Dan said.

"She seems to be a stranger in these parts," Mason observed. "At least nobody seems to know where she came from and why she's here."

"You've inquired?" Dan asked.

He could see that he had ruffled Mason's surface. But the man only smiled. "I didn't ask you here to discuss mysterious ladies," he said. "I doubt that she will prove to be mysterious in the long run. Chances are she'll probably turn out to be a dance-hall girl looking for work."

34

Dan shrugged, although he doubted that. Jennifer Spring hadn't stacked up as the sort who made her living in that profession.

"I'm happy you decided to come and see me," Mason said.

Dan reached into his pocket and drew out the half of the hundred-dollar bill. He laid it on the desk in front of Mason. "You sent this to me," he said.

Mason pushed it back toward him and produced the other half of the bill. "It's all yours, Cameron," he said.

Dan let the two halves of the bill lie on the desk. "For what?" he asked.

"For helping me find out who's back of the damnable things that are happening down in Eagle Basin," Mason said. "And to my friends, Bart and Consuelo Webb."

Dan was surprised. "To the Webbs?" he echoed. "But I understood—"

"I know," Mason snapped. "I see they've already poisoned your mind against them. That fool Vickers boy should have his ears batted down for standing there today and making that idiotic scene against Bart. I suppose Anastasia Vickers has wept on your shoulder and told you that Bart killed her husband. Naturally you believed it. But there's another side to it."

"You mean it isn't true?"

"Of course it isn't true. The evidence was so flimsy the jury exonerated Bart without leaving their chairs. I mean to find out who it is that hates Bart and has hounded him almost into ruin. I'm asking you to help. That money is only the first payment."

"Exactly what would you want me to do?" Dan asked slowly.

"That's up to you," Mason said. "You've been a law officer. Therefore you must know ways of getting to the bottom of this better than I."

"I take it you don't know who to suspect," Dan said. "Or why this person is after Bart Webb."

"That's the blasted mystery of it," Mason said, wagging his head regretfully. "My only hunch is that somebody from Bart's past life is out to make things miserable for him."

"It seems like if it was a grudge from the past it must be an ugly one," Dan said. "I understand there's been night riders and such, women an' children terrorized. And some murders. Ed Vickers was a mighty close friend of mine. I'm told they found the tracks of Bart Webb's prize riding horse at the scene. Ed's widow is scared and is about to pull out of the basin."

"That's the shame of it," Mason said. "I'm going to get Mrs. Vickers a job in the capital. I'll see to it that Lennie gets schooling there."

"He isn't leaving Eagle Basin," Dan said.

Mason frowned. "What's that?"

"The boy has decided to hang on," Dan said. "He's out to get the man who murdered his brother. He's sure it was Bart Webb. I'm afraid he might brace Webb again, like he did after the trial."

Mason slapped an angry hand on the deak. "He's being foolish! I'll have to talk to him."

Dan looked at the portions of the bills on the table, but made no move to pick them up. "It seems to be a job for the sheriff," he said. "He wears the badge. He's got the authority."

"Jim Honeywell?" Mason said scoffingly. "Jim just runs in circles. He couldn't track down a three-legged mule. Either that or he's got an iron in the fire himself."

"How about hiring a Pinkerton, or a Wells, Fargo agent?" Dan asked.

"You would be far more valuable to us," Mason said. "At least they would begin thinking a second time if they knew that Dan Cameron was on Bart's side as a bodyguard."

"You used the word 'they' just now," Dan said. "You seem

to think there is more than one of them out to get Bart Webb."

Mason hesitated, then shrugged. "It has always seemed to me there must be more than one of them."

"You just said you wanted me to act as a bodyguard for Bart Webb," Dan went on. "In other words, you're hiring my gun."

"Now that's hardly the way to put it," Mason said, spreading his hands apologetically. "I'm interested only in seeing that my friend is protected."

"Why not Largo?" Dan asked, with a motion of his head toward the closed door. "That job is more in his line."

"The truth is," Mason answered, "that I feel my own life is in danger because I'm siding in with Bart. I brought in Max to sort of look after me. He's my personal bodyguard."

Dan arose. There was frustration in him, and a deep anger. "You've got me wrong, Mr. Mason," he said. "The truth is that you want someone killed. I've got a hunch you know more about who's back of this deviltry than you want to tell me at this time. I'm afraid you'll have to look a little farther for someone to pull the trigger on him. Killing for pay is out of my line. It always has been. I only killed in my line of duty as a law officer. Good night."

"Now, now, Cameron!" Mason remonstrated. "All I'm asking you is to again help on the side of law and order."

"That I will do," Dan said. "If anyone tries to crowd me down in this Eagle Basin I'll build a fire under him from here to there. But I won't expect to be paid for protecting my rights."

"You're really not serious about settling in the basin?" Mason said incredulously. "Dan Cameron, a sodbuster?"

"That's right," Dan said. "Good night again, Mr. Mason."

He opened the door and walked out of the room. As he had expected, Max Largo was in the hall and had been eavesdropping.

"Kill your own snakes, Max," Dan said, as he walked past the man and left the building.

He felt unclean, sick at heart. All that anyone seemed to want of him was his gun—a gun that would kill. Even young Lennie Vickers had sent not for him but for his gun.

He walked blindly along the sidewalk in this unlighted area and was halted as he found Father Terence O'Flaherty blocking his path. The plump padre had been strolling and carried a walking stick.

"Remember, my son," the priest said softly. "He who sups with the devil must use a long spoon."

The padre moved on by, the thump of the walking stick receding in the direction of the rectory of a steepled church down the street, where he evidently was a guest for the night.

Dan walked on past the plaza, where a single night lamp burned in the depths of the baroque courthouse. Rimrock was quiet. Pioneer Street had grown sleepily deserted, with only the saloons and gambling houses displaying activity.

He entered the lobby of the Stockade Hotel. The sitting room was deserted except for Lennie Vickers, who occupied the sagging cushions of a davenport.

Dan sat down beside him. "I've decided to maybe file on a claim down in Eagle Basin, Lennie," he said.

Lennie's mood shifted from morose brooding to surprise. "Do you mean that?" he exclaimed.

"I mean it," Dan said. "I hope you can give me advice as to the best place to file on, and how to go about it."

"You won't have no trouble findin' a claim," Lennie said bitterly. "The basin's about empty, except fer us, an' two or three old hardscrabble bachelors who don't count anyway, fer they're back more in the hills. An' if you don't mind, my name is Leonard, an' I'd rather be called Len than Lennie. I'm no longer a baby."

"Of course," Dan said. "How far is it to Eagle Basin?"

"We can't make it in one day by wagon," Lennie said. "It's

38

more'n forty miles an' we have to descend the escarpment on a trail that's sure snaky. It'll be close to sundown the second day before we kin make it to Pinedale. There's a stage that runs twice a week an' makes it in one jump, for they got relays, but it's a rough trip on passengers."

"Tell me about Pinedale," Dan said.

"That's the town in the basin. It's only three miles out of Pinedale to our claim. You kin git most anything you need in Pinedale. There are big cattle an' sheep outfits east an' south of the basin that outfit there. You kin travel with us. We came to Rimrock in the wagon an' team. There's plenty of room. We'll likely hit the trail early the day after tomorrow."

"Fine," Dan said. "We better be turning in. I'll need more help from you tomorrow, Len. I'll travel with you and Tansie, but I want to try to find me a good saddlehorse here in Rimrock tomorrow if you can show me where to dicker for one."

"I sure can," Lennie said.

"Good night, then," Dan said, and arose, heading for the stairs to go to his room. He almost collided with another guest, who had just come in from the street. Jennifer Spring. She still wore the bonnet and the veil that hid her features and hid whatever expression might betray her thoughts. She carried a reticule on her arm. It swung against his arm as they met and he was aware that it carried an object of some weight. A pistol, he was sure.

"Excuse me," Dan said, removing his hat.

"My fault, Mr. Cameron. My fault entirely."

They got their keys from the night clerk at the desk. She mounted the stairs ahead of him. Her ankles were trim, the slippers she wore were expensive. She unlocked the door of the room she was occupying, and said, "Good night, Mr. Cameron."

The door closed. Dan heard a key turn in the lock, heard a chair being wedged against the knob as a further precaution.

He moved on to his own room. Jennifer Spring was indeed an increasing mystery. She had not bothered to explain why she was out alone at this rather late hour in a strange town. No doubt that was why she was armed. And, no doubt, she was sure she owed no explanation to anyone, least of all to him.

He entered his room. He started to touch a match to the wick of the lamp, then extinguished it and drew the window shade down, making sure the opening was entirely covered before lighting the lamp. The room had only the one window. Then, a trifle sheepishly, he followed Jennifer Spring's example and wedged a straight-backed chair under the knob.

He lighted a cigar from the supply he had brought in his suitcase, undressed, got into a long nightshirt, and lay on the bed, smoking in defiance of a faded sign on the wall which warned against just such a pastime.

A hand tapped the door. It was Lennie Vickers. Dan arose and admitted him. Lennie was a little embarrassed at the sight of the nightshirt and Dan grinned. "It beats sleeping raw," he said. "What's on your mind, Len?"

Lennie saw to it that the door was closed and spoke softly. "I jest wanted to make sure I heard right. Did you really mean it about takin' a claim in the basin?"

"I mean it," Dan said. "Any objections?"

"You had a powwow with Willis Mason tonight," Lennie said slowly, and let it hang there in the air.

"How do you know that?" Dan asked.

"Maybe a little bird told me," Lennie said.

"A little bird named Father O'Flaherty," Dan said. "You want to know where I stand, don't you?"

"Willis Mason backs Bart Webb," Lennie said grimly. "He ain't no friend o' people like us, no more'n Bart Webb is."

"Willis Mason offered to hire me to find out who's terrorizing the basin," Dan said. "He doesn't seem to think that Bart Webb is the one."

Lennie didn't know what to say for a time. "So?" he finally blurted out.

"I don't sell my gun," Dan said. "To anybody. No more than your brother ever did. But I'm going into the basin to try to find out who's doing the killings. I owe that to Ed—and to you, Len."

Lennie's face lighted up. He drew a long breath. "That makes me feel a lot better, Mr. Cameron," he said huskily. "A whole lot better. I believe you. I'm sorry I been actin' the way I did. Ed always told me how much he thought of you, an' how you two had been like brothers. That makes you sort of a brother to me, don't it?"

Dan extended a hand. "Of course," he said. "Shake on it. Call me Dan from now on. Do you remember me from that time your folks brought you with them to Wyoming to visit Ed?"

"I remember," Lennie said. "I remember just how you looked."

"How did I look?" Dan asked slowly.

Lennie gulped. "You had a gun in a holster. You wore a white shirt and a black tie and a vest with a badge pinned to it, all clean an' neat. Your pants were creased. Your boots were shined. You looked like—well, like I've wanted to look ever since. Like you wasn't afraid of anything, like you would always walk tall and proud."

Dan didn't speak for a space because a lump had come in his throat. "And how do I look now, even in a nightshirt, Len?" he managed to ask.

Lennie hesitated, then blurted it out. "Older. Sad. Lonely. And it ain't the nightshirt. What have they done to you, Dan?"

Dan didn't answer that for a time. "Maybe I'll find the answer to that down in this Eagle Basin," he said. "Now hit the hay and be ready to help me tomorrow."

CHAPTER FOUR

Dan breakfasted with Tansie and Lennie. Afterward, he and Lennie made their way to the government land office which had space in the courthouse. The office had just opened, and the agent, yawning, bored, straggled to the counter and grumpily asked Dan his business.

"I'm thinking of taking up a claim," Dan said. "I've been told there's good land to be had in a place called Eagle Basin that is still open to entry."

The agent's apathy vanished. He blinked at Dan, and apparently realized who he was, news of the appearance of Dan Cameron from Wyoming here in Rimrock evidently having gotten around. He hastily began rummaging through his file of maps, returned, and laid a map book on the counter, turning to a page that he sought.

"There's plenty to choose from," he said. "But as fer it bein' good land is another matter. If anybody asked me I'd say the basin never should have been opened to homesteadin'. 'Bout all it's good fer is range cattle."

"From what I hear there are some other folks who agree with you," Dan said.

The land agent drew back into his shell. "The ones done in red ink are still held," he squeaked. "The black ones have been turned back, the assessment work not finished. The blank sections never was filed on. Take your pick, friend."

Only three claims were penciled in red on the map. A dozen or more were inked in black.

"Maybe I better go down and take a look," Dan said.

"Suit yoreself," the agent said. "There's plenty o' time. Them claims will wait fer you. Good luck. You likely will need it."

Dan turned to leave. Once again he found himself confronted by Jennifer Spring. She had abandoned her dust-coat, wearing a cool, long-sleeved blouse and a tan skirt and slippers, but had again donned the bonnet and the veil that concealed her features.

"Good morning, Mr. Cameron," she said. "We always seem to be running into each other, don't we?"

"You do seem to get around, Miss Spring," Dan responded.

"Both of us are apparently here for the same purpose," she said. "I heard what you said to the agent. I'm also thinking of settling on some good land in Eagle Basin if any is available."

Dan inspected her from veil to slippers. "You, a sod-buster?" he said ironically.

"Why not?" she responded. "I'm a citizen and of age, even though I don't care to tell you the whole truth about that. I'm healthy, not rich, but ambitious."

"There seems to be plenty of land down in Eagle Basin waiting for someone to file," Dan said. "It's yours if you can hold it, Miss Spring, or is it Miss Summer?"

"Spring," she said. "Jennifer Spring. And don't call me Jenny. I don't stand for that, even from a friend."

"A name like that might look nice on a tombstone," Dan said. "They tell me that's the best crop grown in Eagle Basin."

He lifted his hat, and he and Lennie walked out of the courthouse. "Kinda snooty, ain't she?" Lennie commented.

"She must be from around here," Dan said. "At least I got the impression she knows something about this country. Do you know who she is?"

"Never laid eyes on her," Lennie said. "An' there ain't nobody in these parts named Spring, at least to my knowledge.

44

But I got a feelin' she's as counterfeit as a lead dollar. I bet she's up to somethin'.'"

"I've got the same feeling," Dan admitted.

He left Lennie and returned to the hotel, wanting to talk to Tansie alone. He found her waiting for him in her room, evidently expecting that he would come there.

"You really aren't serious about taking a claim in the basin," she exclaimed as soon as the door was closed.

Dan didn't understand her manner. She seemed almost hostile. He had expected that she would be happy to find a friend as a neighbor.

"I'm going down in the basin with you and Lennie to look around at least," he said.

"You must not," she protested. "You—you just don't understand. I'm leaving the basin as soon as I get what things I own together. I want Lennie to leave too."

"I don't think Lennie will go," Dan said.

"He will only get himself killed, like Ed," she said, almost sobbing. "He's headstrong, but he's only a boy. You must talk to him."

"He's changed into a man mighty fast," Dan said. "He's sure that Bart Webb murdered his brother. He thinks that Webb ought to be brought to account." Dan paused a moment. "If Webb did it, I think the same as Lennie," he said.

Tansie burst into tears. She covered her face with her hands and wept. "Don't say that, Dan," she sobbed. "There's been enough—enough killings. Neither of you will ever come out alive."

Dan was taken aback by her outburst. "What I don't understand is how Bart Webb could have done all the things that are laid against him," he said. "From what I've seen of him he looks only like a man pushing sixty who is ranching on a shoestring with a few down-at-the-heel cowhands. What I don't savvy is why Bart Webb suddenly started out not too long ago to run you settlers out of the basin. Why didn't he

45

go at it years ago when the basin was first opened? It all doesn't add up. I—"

He quit talking, realizing that all he seemed to be accomplishing was to further upset Tansie. She flung herself on the bed, weeping violently.

"Now, now!" Dan said, patting her on the shoulder. "This will all work out. Pull yourself together. We'll talk this over some more another time. I'm going down into the basin with you. There must be some way of stopping what's going on."

She gained control of herself. "I'm all right now," she said huskily. "It's just that you don't know what—what you're up against."

"And you do?" Dan asked slowly.

She didn't answer that. She would not meet his eyes.

"I aim to find out," he finally said. "I'm going to try to find me a saddlehorse and rigging and whatever else I need for the trip. Now you get gussied up and do whatever shopping you have in mind. We'll all have supper together and we'll hit the trail in the morning."

She only nodded wearily. Dan left her, carrying with him the belief that she had not changed her mind about quitting her home in the basin. He found Lennie at the livery, where he had poled up the rear wheels of a canvas-hooded ranch wagon and was daubing grease on the spindles after having removed the wheels. The wagon had seen much service, but still looked fit and tough—the reward of care and maintenance.

"Got a hawss lined up fer you," Lennie said importantly. "It's down at Gus Eilers' corral, waitin' fer tradin' day, which ain't till Saturday. Five-year-old gelded roan. Got some mustang in it, but that's a good point in rough country like in the basin. Been rode mostly to saddle, but he's broke to harness too, an' Gus says he's got enough weight to make a good plow horse if eased into it with patience an' plenty of fodder. Jest the ticket fer you when you start sodbustin'.

All you got to watch out fer, Gus says, is this pony's habit o' takin' a nip out of yore rear end if you don't watch out."

Plow horse! That thought set Dan back a trifle, driving home the realization that he might be dedicating himself to an entirely new type of existence, a world that he had always viewed in the past only with the tolerance and loftiness of a man on horseback.

He had been a cowboy, a hunter of big game, a law officer, and at times a hunter of men—all occupations whose members considered themselves several pegs above the toilers who grubbed brush to clear fields for crops and shouldered the roughness of a breaking plow.

He bought the gelding after confirming Lennie's judgment that it seemed sound. He purchased a stock saddle and head-stall, fitting the rigging carefully to the roan, which measured up to advance notices to beware of its teeth. He bought up a few other items, principally of clothing at the mercantile.

That took the biggest part of the day. He had supper with Tansie and Lennie, but Tansie was still somber and without appetite. She had dark circles of sleeplessness under her eyes, and her fingers were nervous. Lennie, on the contrary, was talkative and excited about the prospect of having Dan as their companion and neighbor.

Dan left them after the meal and strolled the sidewalk, smoking one of his cigars. He wanted to be alone, wanted a chance to think. He was puzzled by Tansie's attitude, and frustrated. It was obvious she was in fear of her life. That was because of her husband's murder, no doubt, but it seemed fantastic for her to believe that a woman would be in danger. He kept thinking of her warning that he was inviting death himself by going into Eagle Basin. The weighted holster at his side was now a comfort. He remembered, with pain, the vow he had made to a dead girl, that he would never pack a six-shooter again. He knew, however, that Madge would understand.

He was not normally gregarious, but now a vast loneliness settled on him. It seemed to him that he was back where he had been in the days when he was a marked man as Dan Cameron, the town-tamer. He had been accustomed to being pointed out to strangers and tourists as the notorious killer and to know that his passing on a street was the occasion for nudging and whispering and staring. Notorious—but very, very lonely. A man who walked always with death at his elbow, for he had by the nature of his task made enemies of many lawless, vicious humans. He walked alone once more now that he had donned the gun. Dan Cameron had returned from oblivion.

He entered the biggest and most brightly lighted saloon on the line of gambling houses and music halls. It was named the Golden Lion and had a long polished bar with glittering brass rails and an ornate back bar with a plate-glass mirror and pyramids of wineglasses. Gambling was available at tables at the rear, but play was meager.

Max Largo sat at one of the tables that flanked the bar, which were reserved for drinkers. He had a companion and they had beer mugs in front of them, showing a series of foam rings, indicating that they were not there for serious indulgence, but were nursing their libations.

Largo's companion was Abel Jenkins. Largo was facing the door and was instantly aware of Dan's entry. He must have spoken to Jenkins, but the round-bellied lawyer, who seemed never to remove his rusty derby, did not turn to look. However, Dan had the impression that Abel Jenkins became acutely tuned to his presence.

Dan ordered beer but only toyed with the mug, sipping occasionally, aware that this was not the answer to the mood that gripped him. Another customer entered and barged so close to him at the bar that he was roughly jostled. He turned and was looking into the grizzled, hooknosed face of the ancient cowhand who had been with Bart Webb. Dan stood more than a head taller. As he looked down into the faded eyes and seamed face he knew complete despair and pro-test. He had seen men on the prod before, men who were out to kill or be killed. Above the batwing doors, which still vibrated, he glimpsed the face of the black cowboy who stood there on the sidewalk—listening, waiting.

"So yo're Killer Cameron?" the white oldster said, his voice shaking a little with tension and desperation.

"My name is Dan Cameron," Dan said carefully. "That's what my friends call me. And you?"

"I'm Pat Reilly," the man said. "Tophand at the Circle W. *My* friends call me Bandy. I been with the Circle W nigh onto thirty years. I hear yo're takin' land in Eagle Basin. Or pretendin' to."

"Any objections?" Dan asked.

"Only if you live on slow elk that wears the Circle W brand," Pat Reilly said. "Or cut fences so as to let what few steers we got drift into bogs along the river. Or stampede our horses at night into bustin' their laigs in the coulees. Yeah, I'll object to leetle neighborly things like that. I'll come after you with a gun."

Here was a bitter man who obviously knew that he was in far over his head, but who was going through with it, come what may.

Max Largo, who had been listening from the nearby table, spoke. "Kick the old drunk out of the place, Cameron. He's annoying all of us."

"Jest try it, Cameron," Pat Reilly said. He stepped back a pace, a move that gave him room to draw. He was packing a cap-and-ball pistol in a half-breed holster, the long muzzle projecting along his thigh. The heavy weapon seemed ludicrously cumbersome on his warped frame.

Max Largo spoke jeeringly. "You know you ain't got the sand to draw against Killer Cameron, Reilly. If I was Cameron, I'd turn you over my knee and tan your britches, you old souse."

Largo was trying to force a gunfight. And Pat Reilly had

been drinking. He was drunk enough to be pushed into the trap. "I'll show yuh!" he panted, and reached for the heavy pistol.

Dan was faster. He did not go for his own weapon. Instead he moved in, caught Pat Reilly's arm before he could yank out the gun. He was much the stronger. He twisted Reilly around, forcing him to face the bar, then disarmed him with his free hand.

"Quiet down, friend," he said. "Let's talk this over. Just the two of us."

He was looking at the door, waiting. The black man had moved. He had advanced a pace, partly opening the double swing doors. Then he halted as though settling down again to wait. He wore a gun, but had not drawn.

Pat Reilly was afume with humiliation. "Let go of me, you damned leppy!" he frothed. "Give me back my gun an' we'll go out in the street an' settle this. I might not be as young as you, but—"

A man came charging past the black man into the place. He was Bart Webb. He halted, staring. He was armed, and it was evident his first impression was that Pat Reilly was being manhandled. He started to go for his six-shooter.

"No!" Dan said. His voice was not raised, but it was cold. Very cold.

It halted Bart Webb. He froze, his hand on the hilt of his gun, but going no farther. "Your rider came here asking for trouble," Dan said. "He's not hurt. Take him somewhere and sober him up. Here's his hogleg."

He slid the heavy pistol down the bar to within Bart Webb's reach, and freed Pat Reilly. Stepping back, he stood waiting. He had still made no move toward his holster.

Bart Webb stood for a space, measuring Dan. Then his gaze swung to Max Largo at the table. "Why, Largo?" he asked. "Pat's like one of my family. You were forcing this. Why?"

Largo laughed. "Reilly was the one who kept crowding

Cameron. I wouldn't have let him be knocked off. I'd have taken a hand."

Dan realized then how close to death he had really been. Not at the hands of Pat Reilly, but of Largo. Largo had tried to force a situation whereby he could have shot his target in the back and could have claimed it was to save Pat Reilly's life.

Bart Webb looked from Largo to Dan. "Blood!" he spat scornfully. "That's what both of you wanted. And to see a man die. Two of a kind. Come on, Bandy. Let's get out of here. This place stinks."

Max Largo's harsh laughter followed the cattleman as he almost forcibly led Pat Reilly out of the saloon.

"You were too anxious, Max," Dan said to Largo. "Is it that old grudge from Wagonbox?"

"I don't know what you're talking about, Cameron," he said. "Grudge? Now why would I hold anything like that against you? I admit that if I'd been in your place just now I would have taken care of that old fool. He was asking for it. How many would that have made for you? Or do you bother to keep count?"

"I bother," Dan said. "But I had hoped that I had closed out the list for keeps. Maybe I was being too optimistic."

He walked out of the Golden Lion. Bart Webb and his two riders were already a distance away, on foot. They vanished into a side street. Dan felt sure that it was over for the night at least, as far as Pat Reilly was concerned. Bart Webb had the air of a man who meant to hustle his man off to bed.

Dan kept walking, the bitterness deepening within him. Two of a kind. Bart Webb's accusation kept echoing in his memory. He was being placed in the same category as Max Largo, a man who loved to kill for the sake of killing. He was Killer Cameron, the title that had been given him by a writer for a lurid eastern newspaper.

He found the steps of the Stockade Hotel in front of him and entered the lobby, then mounted to his room to find refuge. He locked the door, removed his hat and coat, and hung his gunbelt over a chair. He lighted a cigar and lay on the bed gazing vacantly at the ceiling, trying to decide his course. Tansie Vickers, he kept telling himself, was right. Eagle Basin was no place for him. The waters there were too deep, too cold. He felt there were factors involved that others, including Tansie, knew about, but that were being kept secret from him. A hand tapped on the door.

He could hear the grandfather clock in the lobby below striking the hour of ten, the chimes soft, musical. He laid the cigar in an ashtray on the stand, reached out, and lifted his six-shooter from the holster. "Yes," he called.

"Are you decent?" a voice spoke cautiously. A woman's voice.

"Tansie?" he replied, surprised. He arose, moved to the door, unlocked it and opened it.

But his visitor was not Tansie Vickers. She was Jennifer Spring. She was taken aback when she saw the gun in his hand, but she pushed past him into the room, peering back over her shoulder as though to make sure she had not been seen.

"I want to talk to you," she said. "Please close the door."

The frown of disapproval that was growing on his forehead brought a little impish smile to her lips. "Your reputation is safe," she said. "This is strictly a business call. May I sit down? It would help *my* reputation if we kept our voices down. They say walls have ears."

He motioned her toward the cane-backed rocking chair, extinguished his cigar in the ashtray, and sat on the bed.

"Could I offer you a cigar?" he asked.

She smiled. "I'm not as tough as you would like to make out," she said. "I was about seven years old when a cousin and myself tried a cigar back of the barn. I've never had the urge since."

She accepted the rocking chair. She had her reticule slung on her arm and Dan was sure it was still weighted. She apparently had just come from her room, for she was hatless, and without the bonnet and veil. For the first time Dan got a satisfactory look at her. She had finely formed nose and chin. She was cheekboned high enough to give deceptive thinness to her face. Her eyes were more hazel than green in this light, and her hair was a shade of rich copper that changed to hammered gold as her head caught the light.

She endured his inspection calmly. "I hope I make passing grade," she said. "Now for the business matter."

She delved into the reticule and brought out a leather wallet. From it she extracted a thin supply of banknotes. She counted out bills carefully and laid them on the stand. "One hundred dollars down payment," she said.

"For what?" Dan asked.

"What I need," she said, "is a bodyguard."

Dan stared at her for a long time and failed to destroy her poise. "What you likely need is a husband," he said. "Pretty girls like you shouldn't be running around loose."

She smiled tightly. "Husbands are easy to find. Men who are worth hiring as bodyguards aren't nearly as plentiful."

"Go back to wherever you came from, get married, and raise a family," Dan said.

"I probably could up the ante," she said, "but something tells me you'd still refuse."

Dan looked at the banknotes on the stand. "Just who is it *you* want killed?" he asked.

She seemed to roll that question over in her mind for a space. "Apparently you've had another offer," she said.

"Not exactly on the same terms," Dan said.

"From whom?" she asked. "And how much was this person willing to pay to have someone murdered?"

"In cash? The same as you're offering."

She sighed. "Well, I can't afford to offer any more. You accepted the other proposal, I take it."

"No."

"Why not?" she demanded.

Dan moved to the door, placed his hand on the knob. "It's time you left, Miss Spring, if that is really your name. Good night."

She remained in the rocking chair. "I apologize," she said. "But everyone says that—that . . ."

She faltered. Dan finished it for her. "That I'm a killer," he said. "That I'm for hire."

She met the issue squarely. "Yes."

"You must leave," Dan said.

"I don't want anyone murdered," she said. "I only want to see to it that I'm not the one who's killed."

"Why would anyone want to kill you?"

"I'm not sure," she said. "I only have a feeling—a fear. A woman's intuition, if you will. You are planning on taking a claim in the basin. When do you intend to go down there?"

"Tomorrow, if we can get organized," Dan said.

"We?"

"I'm going to travel with Tansie and Lennie Vickers."

She arose. Again the impish smile flickered. "I must leave before I wear out my welcome," she said. "I'm sorry I rubbed your fur the wrong way. I'm beginning to believe I misjudged you."

"In what way?" Dan demanded.

"Time will tell, I hope," she said. She extended a hand. "Do we shake on it?"

"Shake on what?" he asked.

"Well, at least we're likely to be neighbors if you are serious about filing on a claim," she said. "I want to be friends. I'm eager to become a settler in the basin. In addition, I would like to travel with you and Mrs. Vickers when you head down the trail. I understand it is quite a rough trip. I bought a wagon and team today. I'm not very good at traveling alone in these parts. I won't, of course, if I'm not welcome."

Dan sighed. "How could I refuse? Welcome." He shook hands. Her fingers were strong, cool, slim. "I won't be a burden," she said. "That's a promise. Good night now."

54

Dan held the door open for her to leave. She peered out before stepping into the hall and believed the coast was clear. But a door opened toward the front of the building and Tansie Vickers' face appeared. She glared with shocked disapproval.

"Good evening, Mrs. Vickers," Jennifer Spring said calmly, and she walked to the door of her own room, opened it, and entered.

Tansie continued to give Dan a withering look, then retreated into her room, closing the door emphatically. Dan shrugged and retreated into his own quarters. He frugally relighted the dead cigar and settled down once again to ponder.

Once more a hand tapped the door. Excitedly this time. "Mr. Cameron! Mr. Cameron!" a voice breathed shakily. "It's me again! Jennifer Spring!"

Dan opened the door. "Come!" she chattered. "Someone's been in my room."

She led him to her room several doors away. She walked to the bed and lifted back the coverlet. "Look!" she whispered.

Dan stared unbelievingly. A knife-blade jutted an inch or more from the pillow. Dan lifted the pillow. The knife was a vicious-looking butcher type, its blade thinned by years of stoning and steeling. The name, Stockade, was burned into its wooden handle. It evidently had come from the hotel's kitchen. It had been thrust through the pillow from the underside, so that only a fraction of the steel point was visible.

"I could see that someone had disarranged the cover on the bed when I first entered the room," Jennifer Spring chattered. "I hadn't bothered to lock the door and had left the lamp burning."

Dan withdrew the knife from the feather pillow. It might have caused injury, or perhaps even death, but both of those probabilities were remote. It had been aimed more at terror—or as a warning.

"Someone seems to be telling you something," he said.

"To stay away from Eagle Basin," she breathed.

"Why?" Dan asked.

She did not answer that. She was pale, but there was no panic in her. "What should I do?" she asked.

"Take the next stage back to wherever you came from," Dan said.

She gazed at him grimly. "No," she said. "But I'll make sure to keep my door locked after this. Your room is within screaming distance of mine, and I can scream real loud. I'll depend on you. That will help me get some sleep tonight, I hope. Good night, Mr. Cameron."

"Nobody seems to take good advice in these parts," Dan said. "I'll try to sleep with one ear open in case you sound off. If it's any consolation to you, I'm sure that whoever put that knife in the pillow wasn't out to kill you, only to scare you."

"He—or they—succeeded in that at least," she admitted. "I'm all goose bumps."

"If you're really going to head down into this basin tomorrow, be ready at sunup," Dan said. "You told me you had bought a wagon and a team. Will you need help? I can send Lennie."

"I can handle it," she said. "The man I bought it from will give me a hand. Sunup, you say? I'll be there. Good night, Mr. Cameron, once again."

CHAPTER FIVE

Jennifer Spring kept her promise. Lennie and Dan were hitching Tansie's team to her ranch wagon at the livery corral when she drove up, tooling a team of tough-mouthed buckskins and a Studebaker wagon that was equipped with a weathered canvas top that sagged over three hoops.

"You bought that wagon from Bill Randall, didn't you?" Lennie said, eyeing the equipment with reluctant approval. "How much did you pay?"

"Two hundred and fifty dollars," Jennifer Spring said lightly. "We started out at four hundred."

"Well, you at least didn't get cheated," Lennie was forced to admit. "Even if you air a woman. Bill Randall's the slickest trader in these parts. He bought that team an' rig from Swede Swenson a month or so ago when the Swede cleared out of the basin with his family. Got it fer a song, but you paid a fair price."

Another vehicle came down the street and halted near Jennifer Spring's equipment. It had originally been a sheepherder's wagon, built with the usual rounded sheet-iron roof from which a stovepipe jutted. A cross was painted on the side of the wagon. It had an adequate team of mules in harness. The driver was the Reverend Mr. Terence O'Flaherty.

"Sure an' I would be happy if I could travel along with you fine folks, being as we are all bound for Pinedale," he sang out in his deep voice. "Provided, of course, there are no objections. I am anxious to get back to my flock, having been gone well onto a fortnight, but the miles will be shorter if I do not have to fare alone."

"Of course, Father," Dan said, smiling. "You're more than welcome, provided you stay sober, don't keep late hours, and promise to stay downwind of me when you smoke that villainous briar pipe that you've got hidden on you somewhere. I learned my lesson about that briar on the stage to Rimrock."

"Conditions accepted," the padre said. "I will absolve you of the sin of ignorance toward a rich and mellow friend, my son."

Tansie was the last to arrive. She was still tugging petulantly at her blond hair and gazing, dissatisfied at her image in a hand mirror she had drawn from her reticule. She was obviously not pleased to learn that Jennifer Spring was traveling with them.

"I really must be a sight," she complained as she let Dan help her to the seat of the wagon. "It's going to be a hot and tiring trip."

Lennie finished storing the last of the belongings, then mounted to the driver's seat beside Tansie and shook out the reins. "We're off," he called. "This is the first time I ever led a wagon train."

Dan mounted the roan, which promptly made a half-hearted attempt to unload him—and failed. He acted as outrider as the cavalcade rolled down the street and out of Rimrock. Father O'Flaherty brought up the rear in his creaking ancient vehicle, which Dan discovered was fitted inside with a small altar at which mass could be recited in out-of-the-way places. The padre occupied a legless padded armchair which was fastened to the otherwise unyielding seat of the sheep wagon. He grinned at Dan and lighted his stubby briar.

The trail carried them past the town's fringe of scattered corrals and farms and truck patches and fenced pastures. It led them into the pine forest where the mists of early morning still lingered. They followed this for miles over an easy and fairly level trail on which they traveled well apart to avoid each wagon's dust.

At noon the trail began to descend gently. Abruptly they came to the rim of an escarpment that dropped almost straight down more than a thousand feet, Dan estimated, to a long talus slope studded with huge boulders.

Beyond lay a rolling basin, extending toward low, jagged bluffs that rose to the east and south.

"Eagle Basin," Lennie said softly. All of them halted to gaze in silence. What they were seeing was pure beauty. It was a gentle country, but not as sizable as Dan had expected, nor as green as the timber through which they had been traveling all morning on the plateau. A river, shrunken by summer to a silvery thread in a wide flood channel, threaded its way among barren stretches of sagebrush and patches of green and apparently left the basin through a break in the bluffs to the east.

The sheer peace and the silence of distance brought an aching longing in Dan. He, the man they called killer, had always been susceptible to loveliness. And here, at last, it lay before him. But beneath that tranquil surface men were being murdered and women terrorized. That brought him jarringly back to reality.

His eyes began picking out details. The roofs of a small town stood in the foreground, the buildings tiny toys at that distance, but distinct in the clear air. A church steeple rose at the far end of the settlement, the cross that surmounted it sending back a glint of gold in the sunlight. At the nearer end of the town was another small church which had a square bell tower.

"My church," Father O'Flaherty said, proudly. "Much of it built with my own hands. And the white-painted church you see nearer at hand has as its pastor the Reverend Mr. George Caldwell, a fine man. He is not of my faith, but we are good friends and labor in the same vineyard. You are looking at the community of Pinedale."

Dan kept looking, the picture growing clearer. Some of the

59

land in the basin had been cleared for crops, but few showed the green of care and water. There was little sign of life, and he became aware there seemed to be only three or four houses among the claims. There were many ugly black dots where homes had been burned.

His gaze moved on eastward, settling on an object that he could not identify. Father O'Flaherty spoke. "The ruins of the mission Santa Rosalia," he said. "Abandoned these many years. What time and weather has not done to the labor of the mission fathers the treasure hunters have accomplished."

"Treasure! Treasure!" Tansie Vickers burst out the words, startling Dan with her bitterness. "I never want to hear that word again!"

She arose and scrambled over the seat out of sight into the interior of her wagon.

"Bad cess to it," the padre said.

Lennie tried to ease the situation. He was pointing. "That's our place there south of town along that freighting trail this side of where Eagle River makes that horseshoe bend. It's just about where the right front arch of a horseshoe would be. You can see it . . ."

His voice trailed off. The mention of a horseshoe had brought back harsh memories. He abruptly picked up the reins slapped them on the backs of the team. "Hike!" he said.

The wagons moved ahead. The easy, meandering trail became a thing of the past. The route pitched down the face of the escarpment in a narrow, winding series of switchbacks that clung precariously to the brushy walls.

Dan finally called a halt. "Len, maybe you better handle Miss Spring's rig," he said. "I'll tie my horse on back of Tansie's wagon and drive for her."

Nobody objected to that arrangement. Jennifer Spring seemed only too happy to turn the responsibility over to Lennie, who, flattered, hastened to take over the reins from her. Dan climbed to the seat beside Tansie and led the way, and the vehicles once more began lurching down the descent.

They moved slowly, the horses leaning back against the breeching much more often than into the collars to hold back the wagons on the downward pitches, a mode of travel that wore on the nerves of both humans and animals.

Dan heard a shrill whistle, and discovered that they were being overtaken. It was the stage from Rimrock. It was a travel-beaten mud wagon instead of the more stately Concord coach, with four horses in harness. It evidently had left Rimrock after their departure. Dan remembered that Lennie had pointed out a relay station back in the timber on the plateau and had said there would be another on the way to Pinedale.

There were half a dozen passengers aboard, two sitting with the driver for the sake of escaping some of the dust. These were Willis Mason and Max Largo. Inside the coach was Abel Jenkins, rusty frock coat and derby hat as usual. With him was the tough-mouthed Pete Slater. The fifth passenger appeared to be a sheepherder by his garb.

The wagons lurched ahead after the dust of the fast-moving mud wagon had settled. "They'll be in Pinedale by nine o'clock tonight," Lennie said, a trifle enviously. "But maybe with not all their teeth. I've heard thet them mud wagons ride like a load of rocks. I wouldn't know. I never been over this trail in one."

They found a spot alongside a tumbling little mountain stream to rest and graze the stock. Tansie spread a tablecloth and laid out cold meat, bread, and preserves. Jennifer Spring helped as best she could but Tansie remained cool and aloof toward her.

After they had resumed the journey Tansie remained silent for a long time on the seat beside Dan. "Exactly who is that woman?" she finally asked.

"Miss Spring?" Dan replied. "That's all I know about her. Just her name."

"Now don't try to act innocent, Dan Cameron," Tansie said caustically. "I've heard how she pushed Clem Coates into a gully and tried to drive the stage into town the other day and how you gallantly took over when she found she had taken on more than she could handle. What sort of a lady would do a thing like that?"

"She's pretty spunky," Dan admitted.

"Spunky? I've got another name for it. I saw her coming out of your room last night. I suppose you've got some excuse for her doing a thing like that."

"She's going to homestead in the basin," Dan said. "She wanted to talk to me about it and ask if she could travel with us today."

"*Homestead?* Her? She acts more like a fancy woman. Going to your room at night! The very idea!"

Dan laughed. "The fact is, she wanted to hire me."

"Hire you? For what?"

"To sort of work around her place, I reckon. And to look after her. She seems to think she'll need protection. I suppose she's heard about what's gone on in the basin."

He waited, expecting more questions. He felt certain that Tansie must have heard Jennifer Spring return to his room to show him the knife that had been thrust in the pillow of her bed. But Tansie apparently had not eavesdropped to that extent. At least she did not mention it.

"She's a fake!" she snapped. "I don't trust her. Not one inch. I don't even think Jennifer Spring is her right name. She's up to something. Either that or she's got her hat set for you. She likely wants a husband."

"Could be," Dan said. "A looker like her could have her pick, I reckon."

After that Tansie again fell into stiff silence. Presently they again heard the thud of hoofs overtaking them. "It's the sheriff, Jim Honeywell," Tansie exclaimed, peering back. "And his deputy, Bill Royce."

Honeywell and his aide came alongside and motioned them to halt the wagons. They dismounted to talk. Bill Royce was a rangy longhorn of a man with a drooping, faded yellowish mustache and hay-rake shoulders in contrast to the compact, black-mustached sheriff.

"I want to palaver with you, Cameron," Honeywell snapped.

"What's on your mind, Jim, me boy?" Father O'Flaherty asked.

"Plenty," Honeywell said. "As if there ain't been enough hell raised in the basin, now we got it spreadin' to Rimrock, beggin' the ladies' pardon fer the slip of the tongue. Clem Coates was murdered last night."

"The stage driver?" Dan exclaimed.

The sheriff's eyes were drilling into him. "Yeah," he said. "The stage driver. Clem was found dead in his bunk in back of the stage station whar he lives when he's in Rimrock. Somebody had druv a pitchfork through him while he was asleep."

A long silence came. "I'm getting the impression that you think I might know something about it," Dan finally said. "Is that it?"

"I ain't sayin' yes, an' I ain't sayin' no," Honeywell said. "You was in on that stunt of settin' Clem afoot after this young lady here who calls herself Jennifer Spring shoved him into a cactus patch. Then you had a ruckus with Clem in town an' mauled him around some. Maybe you figured Clem wasn't the kind of a man who'd forgit a thing like that and would try to even up."

Again there was a long silence, accented by the swishing of tails and the twitching of muscles of the horses driving off flies.

"Are you arresting me?" Dan finally asked.

Honeywell chewed reflectively on the stub of a dead cigar in his strong teeth. "Not yit," he said. "But I warn you not to leave this country till I do some more investigatin'. You've been in trouble ever since you hit Rimrock. How 'bout that bullet what busted the window in Mrs. Vickers' room? You happened to be around when that took place. An' you come within a whisker of a gunfight with Bart Webb an' Bandy

Reilly in Jake Barker's Golden Lion last night. Things seem to happen when fellers like Dan Cameron show up."

He turned and swung back on his horse. His deputy followed his example. "I got to tell Alex Coates about his brother," he said. "It ain't a duty I look forward to. An' maybe you better stay clear of Alex, Cameron. I didn't let them telegraph him the news, fer I wanted to make sure he didn't do nothin' rash."

The two officers rode ahead. "Who is Alex Coates?" Dan finally asked.

"He's the repair man in Pinedale," Father O'Flaherty replied, frowning. "A man of strength and violence. A brawler and a drinker. And a braggart."

Lennie glared scornfully in the direction of the departing sheriff. "Thickhead!" he raged. "As if Dan Cameron would use a pitchfork. A *pitchfork!* M'Gawd!"

They moved on. The slow, rough miles jolted by. The sun cast long shadows that crept across the basin and enfolded the shark-toothed bluffs. They reached the tortuous descent of the talus slope and entered darkening timber, broken by fantastic rock monuments and turrets.

"We should camp here," Father O'Flaherty said as they reached a small flat along a creek which was flanked by pines, cedars, and oaks.

The site had been much used in the past, that fact marked by stone circles where campfires had been built. They positioned the wagons, and Dan and Lennie unharnessed and watered the horses, picketing them on graze. By that time Tansie and Jennifer Spring had a small camp stove set up with dead pine wood crackling. The padre was mixing biscuit dough in the mouth of the flour sack. Lennie built a campfire for additional cheer, and he and Dan helped with what chores they could.

Balmy darkness fell as they ate, and a brilliant moon just past the full rode the sky. After the meal, Jennifer Spring found an opportunity to speak to Dan alone.

64

"It didn't seem to occur to the sheriff that there might be others who were afraid Clem Coates held a grudge, and decided to strike first," she said.

"Namely?"

She showed a small, rueful smile in the light from the distant campfire. "Myself, for one. You know that. After all, I'm the one who pushed that poor man down that hill. Perhaps I was afraid he'd try to pay me back."

"Somehow I can't visualize you as using a pitchfork in a matter like that," Dan said. "A hatpin, maybe. Or a stiletto, but not a pitchfork."

"Thanks for believing there might be a limit to my ferocity," she said. "However, I'm sure Clem Coates had other grudges in his repertoire. And was feared by other men."

"Repertoire!" Dan repeated. "Now that's a nice round jawbreaker. You didn't learn it in Eagle Basin. But you *have* been here before."

"Don't change the subject," she said. "I'm thinking of a little, squirmy-mouthed fat man who always wears a derby hat and has a vicious, selfish mind. I'm sorry now that I didn't let Clem Coates maroon him on the trail."

"Abel Jenkins," Dan said. "Our minds seem to run along the same path."

"Perhaps we should mention this to the sheriff before he gets up enough courage to really try to arrest you," she said. "He intended to, you know, but didn't really have the sand to do it in case you decided you didn't want to be arrested. I think he was also intending to take me into custody."

They let it ride there, for Tansie was approaching, clearly curious as to their conversation. "Time to turn in," Dan said. "It's been a long day."

He and Lennie saw to it that the livestock were strongly picketed. They got their bedrolls from Tansie's wagon and spread tarps and the bedding on dry sand near the creek. Dan was toiling to free himself of his boots when a figure came out of the moonlight. His reaction was to reach for his six-shooter, which he had hung in its holster from a branch.

"It's only me," Jennifer Spring's voice whispered. She was carrying a tarp and bedding. "I hope you two don't object. I just couldn't sleep alone in the wagon. I keep hearing things. I know I'm being a nuisance, but I'm—I'm scared at being alone. I don't want Mrs. Vickers to be disturbed. I think she's already asleep."

"O' course, Miss Spring," Lennie said gallantly. "There's plenty o' room. An' don't you be skeered. I'm a light sleeper. So is Dan. We won't let anythin' happen to you."

Dan could hear the rustling of garments as Jennifer Spring prepared for sleeping in the bedding she laid out nearby. Lennie was snoring within minutes after he had wrapped himself in his bedroll. Dan, never quick to drop asleep, was sure that Jennifer Spring also lay awake.

The night was pleasantly mild, with night birds twittering drowsily in the willows. Occasionally a trout splashed in a pool, feeding on night-flying insects. The coals of the dying campfire formed a small, crimson eye fifty yards away. There was no wind. Dan heard the deeper, soft breathing of Jennifer Spring. She was asleep. He also lay at peace, and soon he also slept.

He was torn out of those depths by a violent sound. An explosive red glare had burst from the campsite, lighting the tops of the willows. Before he could struggle from his bedding the glare faded and was succeeded by the crackling of flames. "My wagon!" Jennifer Spring gasped. "It's on fire!"

The acrid odor of burning kerosene came upon Dan. The horses were rearing and snorting in terror. Some had broken free and were stampeding through the brush. Tansie, belatedly, began screaming.

Dan raced into the camp, his bare feet taking punishment. Lennie was stumbling along at his heels. The canvas hood of Jennifer Spring's wagon was blazing. Charred fragments were

66

drifting in the wind. The thin stubble of grass beneath the wagon was black, smoking, with little tufts of flame still alive.

Dan saw that the damage was still confined mainly to the canvas hood. "Buckets!" he shouted. "Dishpans! Anything! Hurry!"

He snatched up a dishpan and began racing from the creek to the wagon, dousing the flames. Lennie joined him, using a water pail. Jennifer Spring, her dustcoat over her shift, arrived, along with Father O'Flaherty in his nightshirt, and found kettles. Between them they soon extinguished the flames. Except for some scorching and blackening of the wagon bed and loss of the hood, the vehicle and its contents had escaped material damage.

Dan limped away and found his boots. Jennifer Spring was weeping. "Somebody is trying to kill me!" she sobbed. "First that knife in my pillow, then this!"

Tansie joined them. She had dressed hurriedly. She peered closely at Dan and Jennifer Spring. "What are you doing here?" she demanded of Jennifer Spring. "I thought you were sleeping in your wagon when it caught fire. I—"

She didn't finish it, for her voice had turned from anger to scorn. She wheeled abruptly and hurried back to her wagon.

Dan looked at Jennifer and shrugged. "She'll be praying for our wicked souls next," he said.

She was fighting to control her voice, and failing. "Please stay near me," she said. "I'm afraid—terribly afraid."

"Whoever is back of this isn't actually trying to kill you," Dan said.

"What? After fixing a knife in my bed and trying to burn me to death?"

"That fire tonight wouldn't have caused the death of a healthy girl like you who was able to manhandle a person like Clem Coates," Dan said. "You would have got out of the wagon in a hurry. This thing was as counterfeit as that knife business as far as trying to kill you is concerned."

She shivered. "What are you trying to say?"

67

"Somebody wants you to run scared," Dan said. He was eyeing her closely. "Do you know any reason why you're so unpopular in these parts?"

"How would I know?" she responded. But her answer had been a trifle too quick, a trifle too emphatic.

He turned to speak to Lennie, but hesitated. Lennie was standing staring at the blackened wagon. His young face held an expression Dan was unable to interpret. Lennie discovered that Dan was gazing at him, and he forced himself to change expression.

"We better round up the horses," Dan said quietly. But he was still thinking of Lennie's attitude. It was as though young Lennie had stumbled on a thought that appalled him.

The horses had not wandered far and were soon back on picket. The camp began to settle down. "Maybe we better sleep near the wagons," Dan said. "All of us."

"Suit yourselves," Tansie said, climbing into her own wagon. "I prefer a little more comfort than sleeping on the ground. I hope none of you wander in your sleep. I've got a loaded buckshot gun inside and might have a nervous trigger finger."

They brought their bedding into the camp circle and tried to settle down. It was some time before Dan began to drift off. It would have been easy for someone to have stolen into camp with kerosene, touched off the blaze and to have escaped under cover of the noise and confusion. That, no doubt, was the way it happened.

Still—he was aware that Lennie Vickers was still awake. Jennifer Spring had made her bed between them and was asleep.

It was Lennie who stirred at the first hint of daybreak and soon had them all awake. The damage to Jennifer Spring's belongings was insignificant and they soon had her vehicle cleared of ashes and soot and in shape to travel.

Dan took the time to circle the camp, seeking a clue to any rider who might have visited them. He was particularly seeking the print of the giant horseshoe that Lennie had

68

described. But their own stock had spread a maze of hoof-prints over the area. His search was useless.

The sun was well up before they finally pulled out. Dan rode in the lead, following a trail that became increasingly more worn by wheels and saddle stock. They were now on the floor of Eagle Basin. By midafternoon they began to gain more revealing glimpses of the roofs of Pinedale as they topped elevations.

Dan could see that the buildings ran the gamut from rude shacks on the outskirts to well-kept homes and business structures. The largest residence was a pretentious home beyond Father O'Flaherty's church on the east fringe of the settlement. It had many gables and bay windows and was nearly encircled by a wide veranda.

"Willis Mason's home," Father O'Flaherty said, seeing Dan's interest. "A huge house. He must be lonely. He never married, but it is said he built that mansion years ago for a bride who rejected him."

Dan started to ask a question, but something in the face of the padre silenced him.

The trail widened still more, and suddenly they were entering the outskirts of Pinedale. The sun was at their backs, on its way toward the rim of the escarpment to the west. The pace of the leg-weary horses quickened as the animals sensed that feed and rest were near.

As they swung toward the heart of the town they approached a blacksmith shop which had a sizable repair yard that was cluttered with vehicles being mended or in states of abandonment, along with winches, drilling equipment and discarded parts of windmills. A sign over the arch of the wagon gate bore the information:

ALEX COATES
BLACKSMITH — GENERAL REPAIRS
WATER WELLS   WINDMILLS

A group of men was gathered in the repair yard. Seeing the approach of the wagons, they moved into the street. One was Sheriff Jim Honeywell, and with him was his deputy and a massive, bushy-haired man in a blacksmith's sooty, sleeveless shirt and leather apron. Dan surmised that this must be the brother of Clem Coates.

Abel Jenkins was in the group also, along with his man, Pete Slater. Jim Honeywell moved into the clear, and Dan urged his horse ahead, halting to face the sheriff.

"Is this the fella, sheriff?" the big man growled. He had the bulging muscles of his trade, a bulldog jaw, and a stubble of black, wiry whiskers.

"I'll do all the talkin', Alex," Honeywell said. He spoke to Dan. "I've decided to take you into custody, Cameron, till I'm satisfied about some things in connection with the murder of Clem Coates. This here is Clem's brother, Alex. I'm takin' you back to Rimrock to wait action by the grand jury."

"Now that would be inconvenient, seeing as how I just came from there," Dan said. "And also seeing as how I didn't kill Clem Coates and don't know who did."

"Just how do you account for yore whereabouts the night before last?" Honeywell demanded.

"Mostly asleep in my room at the Stockade Hotel like all good people," Dan said.

"Got any proof of that?"

"No. Not unless somebody will testify that my snoring kept him awake. I take it that Clem Coates was pitchforked sometime before daybreak."

"It was long before daybreak," Honeywell said. "We happen to know exactly to the minute when Clem was murdered."

"Is that a fact?" Dan said. "And how did you find that out?"

"One tine of the pitchfork that was pushed through Clem's chest an' stomach busted Clem's silver watch an' stopped it so that we could still read the time. It was exactly two minutes after ten. Where was you about that time, Cameron?"

70

Before Dan could answer, another voice spoke. "Mr. Cameron was in his room at the hotel at that time, Mr. Honeywell."

The speaker was Jennifer Spring. Honeywell turned, staring. She still sat on the seat of the smoke-blackened wagon, holding the reins of the tired horses. "What's that, ma'am?" he demanded.

"You heard me," Jennifer said. "I can testify to that."

"Why air you so danged sure?" Honeywell asked.

"I was there," she said calmly. "I heard the clock in the lobby strike ten just before I went to his room."

"His room? Do you know what yo're sayin', ma'am?"

"Fiddlesticks! Of course I know. But to put at rest any thoughts in your evil old mind, I was there only a short time. Hardly fifteen minutes. Mrs. Vickers can corroborate that, I'm sure."

There was stunned silence for a space. "Is that right, Tansie?" Honeywell finally stuttered.

Tansie's lips were primly set. "Yes," she said curtly.

"Go look elsewhere for your pitchforker, Sheriff," Jennifer Spring said. "Now, if you people will step aside and let us go on our way I would appreciate it. We've had a long journey and I, for one, am bushed."

The sheriff, still dumbfounded, moved aside, and she stirred her team and the wagon creaked into motion. But the big blacksmith barged forward, seized the snaffle of the off horse, and halted the equipment.

"Jest a minute!" he growled. "How do we know these females air tellin' the truth? Any gal, like this one, who'd be brazen enough to admit bein' in a man's room at night likely wouldn't worry about not stickin' to facts. An' we all know what Tansie Vickers was—a dance-hall girl before Ed—"

Dan had slid from his horse. "Take your hands off that bridle, mister," he said.

"Maybe you'd like to try to take it off," Alex Coates replied.

Before Dan could move, Jim Honeywell shouldered in between them. "That'll do fer both of you," he thundered. "Stop it before I have to run the both of you in."

Alex Coates stood, big fists knotted, debating whether to defy the sheriff. His heavy-lidded eyes were wicked under thick brows. He finally decided that this was not the time.

"This ain't over, Cameron," he said. "The sheriff told me who you are. A killer. It was my brother that was murdered in his sleep. I'm told that you an' that gal set him afoot an' stole his stagecoach a few days ago. Then you slugged him later on. I reckon he wasn't lookin'. But I've got some lookin' to do at the story yore lady friends tell, an' I'll look you up ag'in after the funeral. I'm havin' pore Clem's body brought here for burial. This was his home."

Alex Coates wheeled and strode toward his blacksmith shop. Jennifer Spring drew a long, shaky sigh. She glared at Dan.

"For a man who doesn't want to get mixed up in other people's troubles you surely keep a person wondering," she said.

CHAPTER SIX

Dan led the way down the street toward a sign proclaiming the location of a livery. There they arranged for water and feed for the livestock. Tansie and Jennifer Spring disappeared in the direction of stores up the street. Father O'Flaherty parted from Dan, heading toward his church, where he said he had quarters for his wagon and team.

"Peace be with you," he said dryly to Dan as he drove away. "Sure an' you do seem to have been born under the sign of Mars."

Lennie, who had been helping Dan loosen harness and free bits so that the horses could drink and feed, paused and stood watching his departing sister-in-law. Again Dan saw a welling fear and uncertainty in Lennie's young eyes. He placed an arm around Lennie's thin shoulders. "You miss Ed, don't you?" he said.

Lennie softened for an instant, then drew away almost angrily. Dan understood. It was part of Lennie's sudden leap into maturity. He wanted no sympathy. Least of all did he want to be betrayed into displaying softness.

"Course I miss him," he said huskily. "We pulled together purty good. He was more like a father to me than a brother."

"You said this trouble started in the last year or so," Dan said. "Did Ed and Bart Webb have trouble before that?"

"Fact is they was friends," Lennie said. "Ed used to take the rough off young horses an' work roundup at the Circle W to pick up a little extra money. I hung around the ranch house myself, fer Mrs. Webb always had a cookie jar filled an' cold milk in the springhouse. Then everythin' changed. Bart Webb turned ag'in Ed. He turned ag'in all us sodbusters. He swore he'd clean us out of the basin an' make it fit fer cattle ag'in. He sure is tryin' to keep his word."

"You heard him say these things?"

"Well, everybody knows he said 'em."

"Who's everybody?" Dan demanded.

"Shucks, everybody knows him an' his crew started night-ridin'. Old Aaron Crane, who never harmed nobody, was shot while he was eatin' supper with his wife an' kids. Poor Otto Schultz was burned out of house an' home. They killed his plow horse an' his chickens. Other places was shot up. Folks started pullin' out of the basin. Bart Webb was brought into justice's court a couple of times, but he always had an alibi. Ed started packin' a gun."

"*Started* packing a gun?" Dan echoed. "You mean—?"

"Ed never went armed after he came to the basin until jest the last few weeks afore he was murdered. He said he had hoped he was through with that sort of thing. Tansie might be quittin' the basin, but I'm stayin' till I git the goods on Bart Webb."

He quit talking, watching four riders pass by on the street. They were Bart Webb and his wife, along with Pat Reilly and the black cowboy. They evidently were arriving after the long ride from Rimrock. Their horses were head down and worn.

At close range Dan was again struck by the fine posture of Consuelo Webb. She wore a flat-crowned hat in the Mexican fashion, held on her iron-gray hair by a chin strap that framed her high-boned cheeks and soft brown complexion. Her riding skirt was dark and voluminous. She held her chin high, ignoring the group inside the livery yard. But her husband suddenly halted his horse. Dan saw that Webb intended to speak to him. There was challenge and anger in the rancher. But his wife caught his arm imploringly.

"No, Bartley!" she said. "Please!"

74

Bart Webb thought better of it and rode past with his party.

Dan moved into the street, studying the tracks left by Bart Webb's horse in the dust. There was nothing in the shoes worn by Webb's mount to mark them as distinct from the many other prints.

Lennie had watched him. "Bart Webb only rides that big old Morgan at special times."

"Such as at night, maybe?" Dan asked.

"Could be," Lennie answered grimly.

"Are those two old-timers the only riders on Webb's payroll?" Dan asked.

"There are two or three more jest like Bandy Reilly an' ol' Mosely Lee. Bart Webb ain't got many cattle to worry about no more, an' his crew don't draw much in the way of pay. Jest room an' keep. Mose Lee was born a slave. Him an' my brother, Ed, used to do a lot of catfishin' together in the river. Bandy Reilly was quite a roper in his day. They say he was about as good as some of them old-time California vaqueros what could do things with a riata you wouldn't believe."

"Sounds like Bart Webb runs a home for old cowboys," Dan commented.

Lennie scowled, made uncomfortable by Dan's remark. "I reckon they earn their keep by helpin' with his dirty work," he said. "Maybe they—"

He paused. A man had barged from a shabby saloon on a side street and stood belligerently in the path of Bart Webb and his party. The man wore a ragged blue cotton shirt and bib overalls, both of which needed washing, and rundown hide boots. A battered straw hat was sitting aslant on unkempt, sandy hair, and he hadn't shaved in days.

"Somebody run a bunch o' cattle through my truck patch last night, Webb!" the man screeched. "Half of the vegetables I planted to keep me through the winter was trampled down. I worked hard to put in them potatoes an' carrots. I'll make you pay, Webb. You hear me now?"

"I hear you," Bart Webb said scornfully. "Your name is Sealover, I believe. Cal Sealover. In the first place I was miles away, in Rimrock, last night. In the second place you didn't have any crops in that dried-up truck patch of yours. You haven't used an irrigation spade or a hoe since you squatted on that claim. Now get out of my way. You're drunk."

Cal Sealover tried to seize Bart Webb's leg to drag him from his horse. The rancher freed his boot from the stirrup, placed it against his tormentor's chest, and sent him sprawling on his back in the dust.

"Cal Sealover's new around here," Lennie told Dan with distaste for the man in his voice. "He took over an abandoned claim two, three months ago. Stays drunk most of the time."

Cal Sealover staggered to his feet. "Yore day is about over, Webb," he raved. "From now on I'm packin' a gun, an'—"

Dan heard the wicked, snapping sound of a bullet that had passed close by his face. The hard slam of the gunshot came from somewhere back of him. He whirled, ducking aside, his gun already in his hand—a maneuver that had been taught him by harsh experience in the past.

No second shot came. Pinedale's street stood silent and motionless in the soft glow of sunset except for the pitching of the horses along the street. Pedestrians along the sidewalks had frozen in their tracks. Dan could see their eyes, startled, and like his own, roving around in fear of more gunplay.

Cal Sealover was scrambling for cover in the door of the saloon from which he had come. "My God, Webb!" he shrieked. "There's no need fer havin' me killed."

Dan began running down the street, zigzagging, his thumb on the hammer of his pistol, trying to spot any movement that might mean danger. His main objective was a flat-roofed, small structure with a false front that had windows, giving the building the appearance of a second story. Gold lettering on the street-level window identified it as an office.

Dan reached the door of the office and tore it open. A man was rising from a chair at a desk. He was the pudgy, balding Abel Jenkins.

"What—?" Jenkins began to sputter.

Dan raced past him, found a rear door which opened into a cluttered back area. He found himself among ash heaps and the skeletons of worn-out vehicles, along with the shacks of less affluent residents.

He raced to an empty freight wagon, mounted to the high seat and stood on it. That gave him a view of the flat, tarpapered roof of Abel Jenkins' office. It was vacant, but the faint tang of powder smoke was in the air.

Faces were peering from the doors and windows of some of the shacks. "Did you see a man running?" Dan asked.

There was no answer. The faces vanished. The citizens of Pinedale wanted no part of this.

Dan leaped from the wagon and reentered Abel Jenkins' office. That man was on his feet, glaring with righteous wrath. "What do you mean, bustin' into my office like that, Cameron?" he demanded.

Dan was remembering the shot that had been fired in Rimrock into Tansie Vickers' room. That had come from the same type of structure. In both cases an agile man could have lowered himself over the combing at the side of the building and dropped to the ground, waiting his chance to emerge casually into the street while Dan searched at the rear. Dan walked to the door, gazing into the street. He caught a glimpse of Max Largo on the opposite sidewalk, but the gunman seemed intent only on minding his own business, and vanished into a saloon.

Dan instead found himself confronting Bart Webb, who had dismounted and had come striding on foot while his wife and the two riders waited in the street.

Dan answered the question in Webb's eyes. "Nothing," he said. "Whoever fired that shot knew how to get away." He added, "He had practice at it in Rimrock the other night."

Bart Webb's eyes hardened, his jaw squared still more, and Dan braced himself for trouble. Then, once again, his wife intervened, spurring her horse nearer. She reached down, laid a hand on her husband's shoulder. "Come, Bartley!" she pleaded.

Webb reluctantly obeyed, and mounted his horse. He did not look back as he rode away with his party, heading for a trail that led southward out of town into the basin.

Jennifer Spring and Tansie had come hurrying from a mercantile, packages in their arms. "Poor Mr. Sealover!" Tansie chattered. "Now they've tried to kill him too. I'm afraid he'll give up and leave the basin. That's what Bart Webb wants, of course."

Jennifer Spring spoke to Dan. "I'm sorry," she said.

"About what?" he asked.

"Why, about—about you getting involved. It isn't too late. You can take the stage back to Rimrock tomorrow. It only makes the round trip twice a week, they say. You can live in peace somewhere else. That's what you want, isn't it?"

"What makes you think that?"

She didn't answer that. "It isn't your fight. It was that homesteader they tried to kill."

Dan didn't answer that. But she was wrong. That bullet hadn't been meant for Cal Sealover. It had been aimed at him. It had missed Sealover by a dozen feet, but had missed its real target by a whisker.

He stood watching Abel Jenkins emerge from his office, cross the street, and enter a saloon—the same saloon into which Max Largo had vanished a few moments earlier.

Sunset was fading from the sky. "Let's head for the claims," he said.

"What?" Tansie protested. "It's so late. We'll have to unload in the dark."

"The darker the better," Dan said. "Didn't you say it was only about three miles from town to your claim, Len? We can make it in an hour or so. The horses are rested some."

Tansie had her lips set to continue objecting, but Jennifer Spring spoke. "Let's get going. I've got a chilly feeling we're being watched here."

Soon they were on their way, heading out of Pinedale down the trail into the basin. The tracks of the horses Bart Webb and his party were riding, were still fresh in the dust.

"They're goin' on to the Circle W," Lennie said. "It's eight miles east of us." He added, "I'm hopin' Bart Webb an' his outfit will be too tired to do any more ridin' tonight."

They plodded ahead, with Lennie leading the way, handling Tansie's wagon. Jennifer Spring was slumped with weariness on the seat of her vehicle, her team too dispirited to do more than follow the leading wagon.

Dan aroused, sniffing. The odor of burned wood was strong in the air. Lennie swung his wagon off the main road onto a side wagon rut and pulled up after a hundred yards or so.

"Damn them!" he burst out in anger. In the deep twilight Dan made out the burned ruins of what must have been a small house and barn. Little spirals of smoke still rose. The evening wind fingered sparks to life in the smoldering timbers.

"It was the Parsons' place," Lennie said. "They pulled out of the basin a couple weeks ago. Webb's night riders shot up their house a couple o' times. I had sort of figured you'd take over the Parsons' claim, bein' as the house was already built. But now it's gone. The devils!"

Silently, grimly, they returned to the main trail and pushed on. Presently they swung off onto another spur that led to a rise. Topping this, Lennie drew a long sigh of relief. Dan could make out the shape of buildings a short distance ahead.

"At least they didn't burn us out too," Lennie said.

Ed Vickers had built his home in a pleasant clearing well above flood line of a small creek. The house was built of peeled pine logs and was connected to a smaller, single-room structure by a roofed dogtrot. Beyond, as best Dan could make out, was a slab-built barn with a shake roof which served as a wagon shed and hayloft. Cleared fields flanked the house and two stacks of wild hay stood fenced in a pasture.

Tansie entered the house and lighted a lamp. Dan and Lennie cared for the horses while Tansie got a woodstove going and she and Jennifer Spring began preparing a meal.

Entering the house, Dan found the sitting room bursting with cheap mail-order furniture and garish oil paintings. Tansie had always believed she had a future as an artist.

They ate in the kitchen, crowding around an oilcloth-covered table. If any of them noticed that Dan was careful not to silhouette himself against the windows, they pointedly ignored it. They ate in silence.

"I'll bed down outside, of course," Dan said. "In the morning I'll look around and decide where I might want to file."

"Miss Spring kin put up in my place," Lennie said. "It's the spare room. We call it the bunkhouse. It might be mussed up a little, but it's better than sleepin' on the ground. I'll camp with Dan."

Tansie was looking at Dan. "Then you're still set on staying in the basin?" she said argumentatively.

Dan nodded. "At least until I find the answers to some questions."

"Such as?" Jennifer Spring asked.

"If I knew the questions to be asked I'd also know the answers," Dan said.

He and Lennie got their bedding and searched around in the shadows until they found a likely spot on grass that had been cropped short by livestock. Dan spread his tarp and bedroll, making all the sounds and comments of a man at the task of arranging to be comfortable.

Instead of taking advantage of his efforts, he cautioned Lennie not to make a sound and humped their bedding into the semblance of sleepers, and flanked them with their hats and boots. Carrying his pistol in his hand, he crawled into cover nearer the creek, with Lennie following.

Lennie asked no questions, nor voiced a complaint at the probability of discomfort before the night was over. The clatter of dishware came from the lighted kitchen where the two women were winding up the chores. That ended, a light showed in the bunkhouse where Jennifer Spring was preparing for bed. That and the light in Tansie's bedroom were finally extinguished. Silence came from the house, replaced by the endless throb of crickets and the flutter of moths' wings.

Dan lay motionless, trying to sift out any foreign sounds from those of the night. His nerves were on edge. Someone had tried to kill him in Pinedale only a few hours ago. He believed he—or they—would try again, and soon. Someone had burned the abandoned Parson home only the previous night, by the evidence. But Bart Webb had been miles away, as usual, in Rimrock at that time. Then there were the other puzzles: the bullet that had been fired into Tansie's room, the knife in the pillow of Jennifer Spring's bed, and the fire that had damaged her wagon. In the case of the two young women Dan was sure that only terrorism was involved. The bullet that had grazed him only hours in the past had been a different matter.

The question was why? From what he had seen of Eagle Basin it offered little reward, even to a cattleman, for its possession. Certainly not enough to incite a man to hire killers and night riders. He thought of Willis Mason, who was convinced that Bart Webb was innocent. He thought of Lennie, who was convinced that Bart Webb was guilty and the murderer of his brother.

Lennie began breathing deeply. He was asleep. Dan knew that Lennie had been determined to stand vigil also, but youth had prevailed, and he had dropped off in spite of himself.

Therefore Dan alone heard the warning. It was the approach of hoofs, the sounds telegraphed to his ear through the earth. They were so vague that, at first, he was not sure but what they were only the sudden rush of his own pulse. But that ended. He could hear nothing more for a time, but he knew—he felt—that someone was out there in the darkness.

He reached out slowly, drew from the holster the six-shooter that lay at his side. He waited. Lennie sighed and then his breathing deepened.

It came then with the impact of a thunderclap. A six-shooter opened up in the brush and trees well to the left of their position. A second gun beyond the house joined in. That was a rifle, judging by the sharper reports.

The six-shooter emptied. Dan heard the click of the hammer on a spent shell. The bullets had not come in his direction. The assassin had been deluded by the mounded bedrolls he and Lennie had left in the moonlight and had riddled them with slugs.

Dan came to his feet, crouching, and fired a single shot into the shadows from which the flashes of the other gun had come. He heard a strangled snort of dismay, heard a man running through the brush, circling to put the house between him and Dan. Tansie began screaming hysterically in the house, and that helped cover the sounds of the fleeing killer.

Dan ran, trying to locate his quarry. Another shot sounded beyond the house. He believed he saw a moving shadow, but distance and the pale moonlight were of no help. He kept running, circling the house where Tansie continued to scream wildly. No sound came from the bunkhouse, where Jennifer Spring had taken quarters. That brought a chill in Dan's stomach.

Now he heard the terrible sounds of a man strangling in his own blood. He traced these sounds and came upon the body of a man some fifty yards beyond the house. The man was muffled in a ragged slicker and had a black mask over his face. The sounds ceased as Dan crouched beside him, the throes of death ended.

Lennie arrived, breathless. "Stay here!" Dan gritted. "I don't want to shoot you by mistake."

He could now hear the faint thud of hoofs in the distance. Horses were leaving at a gallop. He ran in pursuit. He fell headlong over a dry irrigation ditch and arose, but was confronted by a sagging wire fence from which hung empty cans to deter deer from a garden patch.

He realized that further effort on foot was useless, and knew that by the time he could catch up and saddle his own tired horse his quarry would be far away.

He retraced his steps to where Lennie waited beside the body of the man who had died. Lennie had removed the mask and unfrogged the slicker. Dan peered close in the faint starlight. He looked up at Lennie. "Isn't this—?" he began.

"Yeah," Lennie said huskily. "It's him all right."

The dead man was Cal Sealover, the hard-drinking homesteader who had threatened Bart Webb only the evening before in Pinedale. Sealover's gun lay beside him where it had fallen from his hand. It still reeked of gunpowder. His fingers had gone to the small watch pocket of his vest which he had been wearing beneath the slicker.

Tansie came stumbling through the grass. She had wrapped a bedcover over her nightdress. "What—who—" she sobbed.

"It's your neighbor, Cal Sealover," Dan said slowly. "He just tried to kill Lennie and me. But he was a homesteader, like all of us. Why?"

"You must be wrong!" Tansie choked. "There's a mistake somehow!"

"There's no mistake," Dan said. "There were two of them at least. I heard horses leaving. You might have seen whoever was with Sealover."

"No! No!" Tansie choked. "I didn't see anything."

Dan was remembering the shots he had heard from beyond the house and the silence from the bunkhouse. He began running toward the bunkhouse, a sick chill inside him.

But Jennifer Spring's voice, shrill and thin, sounded ahead. "Cameron! Cameron! Are you all right?"

She appeared out of the darkness. She was barefoot. Dan halted her and wrapped his arms around her, for she was swaying, on the verge of fainting. He steadied her.

"Thank God!" he said. "I was afraid you might have been—"

He didn't finish it. She now peered, seeing the shape of Cal Sealover's body in the starlight. "You?" she asked. There was sudden pity in her as though she was reading the protest and despair that was tearing at him.

"It seems like it," he said. He added bitterly, "Why did it have to be me?"

"Don't blame yourself," she exclaimed. "They came here to kill you—and me!"

She led him to the bunkhouse. She located matches, and with shaking fingers, managed to ignite the wick of a lamp and replace the chimney. "Look!" she said.

The pillow and bedding on the bunk were torn by bullet holes. Across the room a window had been left open on this warm night.

"I heard someone creeping outside," she said. "I rolled out of bed and huddled against the wall before he started shooting through the window."

"Did you see him?"

"No. I was too busy hugging the floor. I heard him running and seemed to hear another man coming up. Then there was another shot and I could hear someone groan, then cough and choke in agony."

Lennie arrived. "It was them damned Circle W killers!" he said hoarsely.

"How do you know that?" Dan asked.

"Who else could it have been?" Lennie answered. "Bart Webb likely was in on it."

"But—" Dan began. He was about to point out some inconsistencies in Lennie's theory. One was that Bart Webb had been heading for his ranch, which apparently was some ten miles east, and was just finishing up a long ride that would not be easy on a man pushing his sixties. Then there was the mystery of why Cal Sealover, an avowed opponent of Bart Webb, would have been in on the raid on the Vickers' place. He decided against making an issue of it.

"Saddle up the roan and ride to town to fetch the sheriff, Lennie," he said. "Honeywell should still be in Pinedale. I'll stay here."

He helped the youth rig the horse and watched him ride away. Tansie was still sobbing and hysterical. He left Jennifer to try to calm her, and carried a tarp back to where Cal Sealover's body lay. He lighted matches and bent over the dead man. Even beyond the frozen pain of violent death there was little in the man's features to arouse pity. Cal Sealover had been rough, tough, cunning.

The forefingers of the right hand were still thrust into the watch pocket of the vest. Dan withdrew the stiffening fingers and a small scrap of paper fell. He picked it up, unfolded it. It was the torn half of a hundred-dollar bill!

The match in his hand guttered out. Dan crouched there for some time, held by surprise, disbelief. He was certain that what he held in his hand was the same half of a banknote that had been offered him by Willis Mason and that he had left lying on Mason's desk in Rimrock.

Jennifer Spring was approaching. She had dressed in skirt, blouse, and shoes. She had a rifle slung under her arm. Dan refolded the bill and thrust it back in the watch pocket from which it had fallen. Cal Sealover's last instinctive gesture before death had been one of greed—an attempt to protect blood money that had been paid him.

"What is it?" she asked.

"I'm not sure," Dan said. "I'm sure of only one thing. You're taking the first stage out of this country."

"And you?"

"I'm sticking around for a while," Dan said.

"To be killed?"

"To find out why I'm only worth a hundred dollars dead," Dan said. "After all, I have my pride."

"What are you talking about? What has a hundred dollars got to do with it?"

He was on the point of telling her about the torn banknote, then decided against it. After all, Miss Jennifer Spring, if that was her real name, presented some puzzling questions in her own right. For one thing, there was the matter of her real purpose in appearing in Eagle Basin in defiance of attempts to frighten her, then kill her. Her pose as a desire to be a homesteader hardly held water.

She stood waiting. When he did not answer, she sighed. "You don't trust me, do you?" she said.

"Should I?" Dan replied.

"Yes," she said fervently. "Oh, yes. I have the feeling that we must stand together—or die together."

Dan drew the tarp over Cal Sealover's body. "I'll stand watch over him," he said. "You and Tansie might as well try to get some rest. Sleep if you can."

"Sleep?" she echoed wryly. "After all, what kind of nerves do you think I have? It isn't every night that somebody shoots up my bed with me supposed to be in it."

"Or plants a knife in your mattress, or tries to burn you up in your wagon," Dan said. "You should be getting used to it. After all, you've used up three of them."

"Three of what?"

"They say a cat has nine lives."

She glared at him. "So I'm a cat? I should use my claws on you."

"I'd prefer to know who you really are and why you came here."

She ignored that. Her voice became grim. "Forget your infernal pride, Daniel Cameron. You're the one who should get out of this country. You've got nothing to hold you here."

86

"But you intend to play out your hand, whatever it is," Dan said. "Is that what you're telling me?"

"Yes," she said flatly.

"We can be married in the morning," Dan said.

"What?"

"Keep your hair on," Dan said. "It won't be for real, of course. But that will be between just the two of us."

"Well I never!" she gasped. "Just what makes you think I would do any such thing?"

"I told you in Rimrock that what you needed was a husband, not a bodyguard," Dan said. "Remember?"

"You can't be serious," she exclaimed, eyeing him suspiciously down her nose. "What are you up to?"

"I *am* serious," Dan said. "You *do* need a bodyguard. You can't deny that after what happened tonight. We seem to be in the same boat. You said we ought to stand together. If we went through a marriage ceremony it would keep folks from talking when they found out I was hanging around all the time. It would be in name only, of course, and we'd call it off as soon as things straighten out."

"You were married once before," she said slowly. "Your bride was killed on your wedding day as you came out of the church at Wagonbox, Wyoming. She saw the killer before he fired and moved in front of you and took the bullet."

"How do you know these things?" Dan asked huskily.

"It was in the newspapers," she said. "Dan Cameron was famous, you know."

Dan did not speak. The memories were too poignant. "She must have loved you very much," Jennifer Spring went on, her voice moist, tender. "Very, very much. *She* trusted you."

Still Dan could not speak. He was remembering the desolation of it. Madge had died because of a grudge. Now, at his feet, lay the roots of a new hatred, a new feud, a new path to more killings. To kill or be killed. And he did not even know, of all the strangers who had come into his life in the past few days, which were his enemies and which were

87

friends. Except one. He believed in this girl who stood at his side and who called herself Jennifer Spring.

"There must be a better way," she said. "That kind of a marriage isn't—isn't what a girl would have in mind."

CHAPTER SEVEN

Dan left Jennifer Spring to stand vigil and circled the house. He had his six-shooter in his hand, and was tuned to every small sound around him in case an enemy remained in the shadows. He heard only the chirp of crickets and the flutter of moths.

He located a spot where horses had been tethered at a considerable distance. They had been there for some time, judging by the droppings. In the moonlight he could make out the tracks left by the animals departing at a gallop and felt that one of the mounts had an empty saddle and was being led. He could not make out anything of significance in the hoofprints in the vague moonlight.

He returned to Cal Sealover's tarp-covered body. Jennifer was waiting. She had donned a heavy saddle jacket, for the past-midnight chill was moving in. She carried her rifle.

"I'll stay here with you," she said.

Daybreak had arrived when their wait ended. Sheriff Honeywell and Bill Royce came riding up the trail, accompanied by Lennie. Following them was a ragged string of a dozen or more townspeople who had been awakened and had tagged along to take part in this new sensation.

Bringing up the rear was a rickety old Army ambulance with a bony team in harness. It was driven by Abel Jenkins, who, it turned out, was the deputy county coroner, stationed at Pinedale. Jenkins tried to take charge of proceedings, but Jim Honeywell would have none of that, and scowled him into silence. The sheriff's expression was cynical as he listened to the accounts Dan and Jennifer gave. He pulled back the tarp and closely inspected Cal Sealover's body.

"Slug in the laig wasn't likely enough to stop him," he commented. "But that one in the back was dead center. The feller didn't do no more runnin' after that hit him."

"What?" Dan exclaimed. "He was hit *twice?* I took it for granted—"

He didn't finish it. Honeywell was watching him shrewdly. "Yeah," he said. "You mentioned you only shot once. I reckon you lost count in the excitement. Or maybe you wanted to make sure of him after the leg wound downed him. There's powder burns around this one in the back."

Dan looked at Jennifer. She was confused, puzzled. He was remembering the cry of pain that had come after his single shot, and was remembering the second shot later on— from the gun of someone else. He decided to keep his own counsel for the time being.

Honeywell walked to the house to talk to Tansie. Dan could hear her hysterical voice. Then the sheriff entered the bunkhouse to inspect the bed where Jennifer had been sleeping.

A new arrival joined the group of bystanders. He must have come by way of the creek brush, which offered a shorter but rougher route across fields. He was Alex Coates, the town blacksmith, riding a gray horse that needed currying.

"Who is it?" Coates asked, indicating the body.

"That nester named Sealover," someone volunteered.

"What?" Coates exclaimed. "Another sodbuster gone? Ain't it about time we got a rope an' put an end to these murders? We all know who's back of it."

"That'll do!" Honeywell thundered as he came lumbering back to the group. "I heard that, Alex. There's goin' to be no lynchin' in my jurisdiction. Nor even any talk of it. I'll handle this legal."

He glared accusingly at Dan and Jennifer. He failed to

glare them down. "You two pull together mighty well, don't you?" he said.

"What do you mean by that?" Dan demanded.

"First she gives you an alibi for Clem Coates's murder, an' now both of you back each other up in tellin' this yarn about how Cal Sealover tried to shoot up your camp."

"Are you saying we're lying?" Jennifer demanded angrily.

"I ain't sayin' one way or the other," Honeywell answered. "But don't either of you go anywheres till I've done some investigatin', an' the inquest is held."

"Are you trying to say we might have killed Cal Sealover?" she exclaimed. "Why, he was a homesteader too. Why would we want him dead?"

"I wouldn't know," Honeywell admitted. "Abel, you take charge o' the body. We'll hold the inquest in town as soon as we kin scare up a panel. Everybody else stay whar they air. I don't want a lot o' fools stampedin' all over the vicinity, tramplin' out tracks."

"You'll find where horses were tied up there in the brush last night," Dan said, pointing.

"I don't need none o' yore help," the sheriff snapped. "Come on, Bill."

He and his deputy headed away and began quartering the area. They crossed the small creek and disappeared into the brush. After a time the sheriff appeared and lifted a shout. "Come here a couple of you! You, Jake Smith an' Will Clark. An' you too, Abel. I need witnesses."

Dan and Jennifer followed the three who had been named. Lennie also trailed along. "You three stay back!" the sheriff screeched, but they ignored the order and Honeywell did not press the issue.

The officers waited where they had found the spot at which the horses had been tethered. Honeywell motioned the group to follow and led the way through the brush. "Take a look, men," he ordered the three who had been summoned. "A good look." He glared at Dan and his two companions. "You three stay back."

Dan did not heed. He moved in, peering over the shoulders of the witnesses, who were crouching, gazing at what the sheriff had found.

The departing horses had crossed a short marshy stretch which the stream had invaded during a recent rainstorm. Water had filled hoofprints near the firmer margin of the soft ground, but there were three marks that were still sharp and distinct. The horse that had worn those shoes must have been of extraordinary size and weight. Dan could not recall ever having seen marks of bigger shoes.

Lennie crowded in, peering. His Adam's apple bobbed in his thin throat. "Bart Webb's horse ag'in," he said. "That proves it. That fool jury let him go the other day because they didn't have the guts to hang a man because of a horse-shoe print. I reckon you got him dead to rights this time, Sheriff. Ain't you goin' to ride over to his ranch an' arrest him?"

"When I want advice from a turkey-necked yearlin', I'll turn in my star," Honeywell snarled. He glared at the men he had summoned as witnesses. "You see now why I brung you here. Look it over keerful. You'll be called on to swear to it at the inquest, an' likely in court when Bart Webb is goin' to be tried ag'in fer murder."

Honeywell suddenly jerked his six-shooter from its holster. He jammed its bore into Dan's stomach. "I'll just take yore smokepole fer safekeepin'," he said, lifting Dan's gun from his holster and thrusting it in his belt. "An' you might as well let me take keer o' yore rifle, lady, in case you git nerv-ous an' shoot somebody."

Jennifer handed over the weapon. "Are we under arrest? Why?"

"I ain't sayin' I'm arrestin' you, but I ain't lettin' either of you git out of my sight till I git some questions answered," Honeywell said.

92

"Such as what?" Dan demanded. "Are you trying to say we were in cahoots with somebody to get this man killed?"

"I ain't sayin' anythin' yet," Honeywell answered. "A'ter all, Cal Sealover was a homesteader, an' it's homesteaders that have been on the receivin' end of tough luck here in the basin lately. Neither you nor this female stack up to me like sodbustin' was yore dish."

Jennifer started to voice a scornful protest, but Dan motioned her to be silent. "We'll wait for the inquest," he said.

He was watching Cal Sealover's body, particularly the vest pocket that contained the folded portion of banknote. But as far as he could see, the fragment was still there when Abel Jenkins covered the body with a sheet and the men helped lift it on a stretcher and into the ambulance. Still, Dan remembered that he had been away for a time, following the sheriff's search in the brush.

The cavalcade was soon on its way to Pinedale in the wake of the ambulance. Dan had hooked Jennifer's team to her wagon, and handled the reins, with Jennifer at his side. Jim Honeywell sat on a box in the bed of the wagon in back of them, his pistol close at hand. Lennie was following the wagon, riding Dan's roan.

"Maybe you better go back and stay with Tansie," Dan said to the youth.

Tansie was standing in the door of the house watching the group pull out. Lennie looked back. "She'll be all right," he said. "She's always all right."

Arriving in Pinedale, Dan and Jennifer were taken to the small office that the sheriff used when in Pinedale. There was a cell room at the back, but Dan was not placed under lock and key. He was warned by the sheriff that at present he was only being held as a material witness. Jennifer insisted that she also be held at the office. "After all, it looks like if Mr. Cameron is guilty, then I'm guilty also," she said.

"Yo're a cool one," Honeywell said reluctantly, leaving

the office, telling Bill Royce to keep guard over the two suspects.

Dan moved to a window and watched Cal Sealover's sheet-covered body being carried on the stretcher into a furniture store down the street.

"Ike Hoskins' place," Bill Royce explained. "He's the undertaker. Only one we got."

Willis Mason appeared on the street and came striding to the jail office; Bill Royce admitted him. "I just found out what was going on, Cameron," he said, extending a hand. "I came to offer any help I can. I'm a lawyer, you know." He looked at Jennifer and added, "I've never had the pleasure of a formal introduction to this young lady."

Dan didn't seem to notice the extended hand, and Mason let it fall to his side. "Jennifer," Dan said, "this is Willis Mason, who tells me that everybody is wrong about Bart Webb. Mason, this is Miss Jennifer Spring."

"A pleasure," Mason said, bowing. "A real pleasure, even under these circumstances. As I was saying, I am ready to represent you young people legally."

"If we need help we'll let you know," Dan said. "I doubt if it will come to that."

Willis Mason was evidently not accustomed to being abruptly dismissed. He started to frown, then shrugged. He bowed and turned to leave. "I'll probably see you at the inquest," he said.

Through the window Dan watched Mason head back toward his home on the fringe of town. He lingered at the window until the men who had carried Cal Sealover's pallet into the undertaking establishment had reappeared. They drifted away along with the bystanders who had gathered. The interest was over for the moment, at least until the inquest was called.

"I'd like to take a look at Cal Sealover," Dan said to Bill Royce.

"What? What fer?"

94

"I promise not to run out on you, Deputy," Dan said. "You can stick with me every minute. And it won't take much more than a minute."

Bill Royce protested that the sheriff would raise hell, but he finally consented, mainly out of curiosity. He and Dan left the office and walked toward the furniture shop. Jennifer had started to follow, but Dan had said, "An undertaker's shop is no place for a lady."

Ike Hoskins was busy in a small room off the main funeral parlor at the rear of the sales room. He had removed the clothing from Cal Sealover's body, and the garments were hanging on wall hooks. Hoskins drew a sheet over the corpse when he found he had visitors. He was an emaciated, sad-faced, elderly man with bony features.

Dan moved to the hanging clothing and ran his fingers into the watch pocket of Cal Sealover's vest. It was empty.

"Did you find anything of value in his clothes?" he asked the undertaker.

"Nothin' but a couple of dollars an' a tobacco pouch an' such," the man said. "Abel Jenkins kin verify thet. He acted as witness an' listed what possession there was."

"All right," Dan said. He turned and walked back to the jail office with the mystified Bill Royce asking questions, which he ignored.

Jennifer also was nettled when he failed to respond to her obvious curiosity. She fell into injured silence.

CHAPTER EIGHT

It was midafternoon, and Dan and Jennifer had eaten dinner at the county's expense at the hotel before Jim Honeywell had rounded up a panel. He led them to the furniture store, where a space had been cleared, with chairs for the jury, and spectators occupying items that were for sale in the long room. Cal Scalover's sheet-covered body was in sight through the door that opened into the small side room. The place filled to standing room in short order.

After the jury of seven men was sworn in, the first witness was Pinedale's doctor, who was addressed as Doc Berrington. It developed that Abel Jenkins was not a doctor, although he held the political office as deputy coroner, but had to depend on Berrington for expert testimony.

Berrington testified that the deceased's death was due to a bullet in the back, which had shattered the heart and a portion of the lungs. Another bullet wound in the leg was serious but would not necessarily have been fatal.

"Mighty good shootin' at night," the doctor volunteered. "Feller who did that was handy with a gun."

"Some men have reputations as dead shots," Abel Jenkins, who was conducting the inquest, said.

"I believe that's been said before," Dan spoke.

"You'll git yore chance to talk," Jenkins snapped. "An' right now. I now call on you to take the oath, killer."

"My name is Cameron," Dan said. "See to it that you use it from now on. I ask Dr. Berrington not to leave this room. I have some questions I want to ask him."

There was a commotion at the crowded door. Bart Webb had entered. He shouldered his way through the spectators and reached the cleared space. He was followed by his wife and by Willis Mason.

The rancher faced Jim Honeywell. "I understand you want to see me, Sheriff?" he said. He wore the common garb of a working rancher: denim jacket and britches, leather cuffs, a limp range hat, worn boots. He carried a six-shooter in a scarred holster which hung from a wide belt. His wife apparently had mounted hastily also, for she had on a pleated cotton skirt and a waist that bore a smudge of flour as though she had left an unfinished baking. She had wound a scarf around her graying hair. She looked neither to the right nor to the left, but Dan saw that there was fright in her dark eyes.

Willis Mason spoke. "I will represent Bart in legal matters, Jim."

Events had moved faster than Honeywell could cope with. He stood flustered. "Now, now, take it easy, Bart," he stuttered. "This here is an inquest, not a trial. We're jest tryin' to git at the bottom of things. This here man, Dan Cameron, is about to tell how he killed Cal Sealover last night."

Men scrambled to clear a place for the Webbs to sit. Dan watched both of them measure him swiftly, carefully, as though they were asking themselves a very urgent question. Their eyes swung to Jennifer Spring. It seemed to him that she was studiously avoiding their gaze. He also had the impression that there was great concern in Consuelo Webb's expression.

Dan moved to the center and briefly told his story. Lennie, who apparently had been kept under guard at the hotel, was sworn in and corroborated the details of the shooting.

"Mrs. Vickers ain't in no shape to testify," Jim Honeywell said. "Her testimony ain't vital right now, fer she didn't see anythin', bein' as she was in the house when the gunplay took place."

Dan was not cross-questioned. Honeywell offered his own evidence. "We scouted aroun', me an' Bill Royce, an' found where two horses had been left in the brush beyond the Vickers' place," he said. "I'd say only two horses left at a gallop, an' that one of them was bein' led. I take it that was the one Cal Sealover rode afore he was killed. We found tracks."

"What kind of tracks?" Abel Jenkins demanded quickly.

Honeywell shot a nervous glance at Bart Webb. He had to clear his throat several times before he could answer. Dan began to realize that the sheriff and Bart Webb were old friends.

"There was a lot of tracks on top of each other," Honeywell finally said. "But we found some clear prints in boggy ground."

"Describe the prints," Jenkins said.

"They was made by a mighty big horse," the sheriff said reluctantly.

"Have you ever seen the horse that makes tracks like that?" Jenkins went on relentlessly. "If so, name the owner."

"Wal, Bart Webb's big Morgan wears shoes that big," Honeywell admitted. "The horse he calls Sultan."

Bart Webb half rose, his seamed face pallid. Then he paused, the enormity of it coming home. His wife was ashen also. She gripped her husband's arm, protectingly. "That's a lie!" the rancher exclaimed.

"You keep quiet, Webb!" Abel Jenkins snapped. "I seen them hoofprints with my own eyes. So did Will Clark an' Jake Smith. They're here in this room. Ain't that right, boys?"

Dan spoke before the two men could answer. "That's right. I saw them myself. There's only one thing wrong. They were *fresh* prints. Water was still oozing into them, but all the other hoofprints were water-filled. These of the big horse hadn't been there long. But the shooting happened hours earlier."

The room went pin-drop quiet. Honeywell finally spoke. "Air you tryin' to say someone planted the shoe prints to make it look like Bart Webb had been there with Cal Seal-over?"

"This feller is lyin!" Abel Jenkins shouted. "Remember, men, it was a homesteader that was killed, just like Ed Vickers was murdered a couple of weeks ago. An' by a man ridin' that same horse. An' remember that Cal Sealover made threats ag'in Bart Webb only the same afternoon, an' branded him as a range hog an' a killer. Well, there's other killers around. Looks like we got one right here in this room. His story about how Cal Sealover was killed don't hold water with me."

"There are a lot of other things wrong with your case, Jenkins," Dan said. He addressed the waiting doctor. "You held an autopsy on the body of the deceased, I believe. You testified that death was caused by a bullet in the back. Did you recover the bullet?"

"Dang right I did," the doctor said, bristling. "Here it is." He drew from his pocket a slug. Dan motioned to him to hand it to Honeywell.

"What kind of a bullet is that, Sheriff?" he asked.

"It's a rifle slug," Honeywell said slowly. "A thirty-eight, I'd say. Deer gun."

Dan addressed the doctor. "And the other slug in the leg that you said would not have been fatal? Do you have it?"

Berrington numbly produced the other bullet and handed it to the sheriff. Honeywell peered for seconds. "A forty-four," he pronounced. "Maybe a forty-five. Too smashed to be sure. But it's one or the other."

"A forty-four," Dan said. "You can verify that by looking at my gun. I fired only one shot, remember. The bullet that killed Cal Sealover came from someone else's gun. Likely the man who rode with him to raid us. He didn't want Sealover to live to talk."

Again the frozen silence. Abel Jenkins had nothing to say. The sheriff spread both arms helplessly. He spoke to the jury. "Guess we was wrong. Cameron had only a six-gun, an' there was still four live ones in it, along with a safety empty. It hadn't been cleaned."

"How 'bout this here gal?" Abel Jenkins screeched, finding his voice. "She was packin' a rifle when we got there at daybreak. Ask her whar she was when the shootin' took place."

"I was trying to hide under my bed in the bunkhouse," Jennifer said.

Laughter swept the room. Abel Jenkins was silenced. The jurors did not ask to leave the room. They looked at each other and nodded. The man they had named as foreman gave the decision. "We find that Calvin Sealover was done to death by a person or persons unknown."

Dan started to escort Jennifer Spring out of the room through the press of onlookers. Jim Honeywell came pushing through and intercepted them. "I ain't satisfied with this," he rumbled. "I want to know where I kin put my finger on you two at any time I want. Whar will that be?"

It was Jennifer who answered. "Well, before the evening is over it will be at some place where we can get married, provided we can get a license and find a minister."

"Married?" The startled sheriff's heavy voice boomed out the word. The shuffling of feet ceased. Heads turned, eyes gawked at Dan and Jennifer.

"Provided the offer is still open, Mr. Cameron," she murmured.

"Are you sure?" Dan asked.

"Yes," she said soberly. "As I said before, we two seem to be in this together all the way."

Dan took her arm again and they moved ahead. The pop-eyed bystanders hastily made a path for them. All but two. Bart Webb and his wife did not move, blocking their way. They looked shocked, puzzled. Consuelo Webb seemed particularly upset.

"Excuse us," Dan said. Consuelo Webb lifted a hand as though to halt Jennifer, then thought better of it, and she and her husband stepped aside without speaking.

Dan hurried Jennifer outside. "Act like a happy bride," he gritted in her ear. "Instead of looking like you'd just got some very bad news."

"It isn't every day that I get married," she murmured. "I'm still not so sure it's an intelligent idea."

"You said it yourself," Dan replied. "We stick together or hang together. It's that simple."

"How romantic," she sighed. "I've always had other plans. But I fear you're right. Your responsibilities—and mine—extend no farther than to see that neither or both of us are murdered. This is to be a marriage in name only and is to be annulled as soon as possible. Understood?"

"Understood," Dan said. "Now to find a preacher and get it over with."

"Not so fast," she said. "Getting married in a calico dress and dusty riding boots isn't what I had in mind."

Jim Honeywell and other bystanders were trying to eavesdrop. She put her arms around Dan's neck and drew his head close so that she could whisper to him. "We must make this look real," she murmured. "We both must spruce up. If you need money to buy a shave, a bath, and clothes, I can stake you."

"I can handle it," Dan said. "But it'll likely take me an hour or so to get ready."

"An hour?" she exclaimed. "Good heavens! I'll need a lot more time than that. My hair is a sight. I've got to shop for the right things to wear. I must get started."

It did take longer than an hour. Much longer. Dan first rented rooms at the Pioneer Hotel, sharing his with Lennie. Then, with Lennie in tow, he made his way to a mercantile, where he found a dark suit that fitted fairly well, along with a white shirt and tie and black shoes. He outfitted Lennie with a new dark suit and a shirt with a stiff collar and tie that made Lennie's jaw bulge.

Then they patronized a barber shop that had baths for hire. Dan was sitting in the barber chair having his hair trimmed and lather on his face, while Lennie splashed in a tub in the back room, when he saw Abel Jenkins walk past the shop, accompanied as usual by his shadow, Pete Slater.

On a hunch Dan rose from the chair and moved to the window, the white cloth trailing. He watched the two men cross the street a block away and enter Alex Coates's blacksmith shop, where a hammer was ringing on an anvil. They were swallowed by the deep shadows in the shop. The metallic music ended.

Dan returned to the chair. "Quite a feller, that Abel Jenkins," the barber said. He was a soft-spoken, mild-mannered man in his sixties named Joe Tracy. "Abel's got a finger in most every pie around here. Sells land, earns lawyer fees, picks up money as deputy coroner. He takes care of things fer Willis Mason when Willis is down at the capital or up in Rimrock politickin'."

Dan became alert. He realized that Joe Tracy was trying to tell him something. "Abel ain't as harmless as he tries to make out," Joe Tracy went on. "He's cut up a few folks in knife fights in his time. Killed one feller. He's made a lot of people real mad at him in these parts. He brung in a plug-ugly named Pete Slater to act at his watchdog. I've heard that Slater's done time for gunplay in Texas in the past."

Two more men strolled by. They were Bart Webb and Willis Mason. Mason carried a walking cane and wore stylish garb. He and Bart Webb seemed involved in serious discussion.

Joe Tracy finished with the razor and towel, and wisped away the white cloth from Dan's shoulders. "I never thought I'd live to see the day when them two would let the past be bygones," he remarked.

"They've not always been friends?" Dan asked.

"There was a time when folks looked around for cover whenever them two was in town at the same time," Tracy said. "Goes back a lot of years to when they was young hellions, hot-blooded an' wantin' the same thing."

"Such as?"

"Such as the *señora* Consuelo Valdez. She was a tearin' beauty in them days. Still is, if you ask me. She's Consuelo Webb now. Her father, Manuel Valdez, came into the basin with his bride in the early days, an' started ranchin' at the east end of the basin. Consuelo was born there. Bart married her when both of them was about twenty. The Apaches were still raidin'. Bart went off to war, an' Consuelo ran the ranch, for her parents both passed away about that time. They're buried at the ranch, which is now called the Circle W. So are Bart and Consuelo's two children. They died young. Consuelo never really got over it. They've had hard goin' there, what with one thing an' another. Consuelo had pledged thet she'll never part with the land where her kin are buried."

"You said that Willis and Bart Webb weren't always friends," Dan said.

"They fought a bloody fistfight here in the street one day, years ago. Neither would admit it, but it was because Consuelo had married Bart an' turned Willis down. There was bad blood between them for years, but it looks like they've smoked the peace pipe. Willis is about the only person who has stood up for Bart this past few months agin all the bad talk that's been passin' agin him."

"By whom?" Dan asked.

Joe Tracy decided he had said enough. He used a whisk broom on Dan's shoulders. "Lennie's finished scrubbin' hisself," he said. "There's still plenty o' hot water in the boiler. As soon as you clear out I'm closin' shop fer the night. I don't want to miss whatever else happens—'specially your weddin'."

"The wedding is going to be private," Dan snorted. "If you want entertainment, find a circus."

He splashed around in the big tub of warm water and toweled while Lennie was having his hair cut. He dressed in his new suit and shirt and gazed into the mirror as he knotted the new string tie. He stood straighter and inspected his profile.

"Don't git to admirin' yore shadow so that you forgit to look over yore shoulder now an' then," Lennie sniffed.

Jim Honeywell had returned Dan's gun and belt to him. He stood for a time gazing at it where he had hung it on a chair. Then he slowly strapped it on. He was aware of Lennie's grunt of approval.

Lennie tried not to show it, but he was mighty proud of himself after he had gotten into his new togs. "You're growing into the image of your father," Dan said.

They walked to the hotel and mounted the stairs. Dan tapped on the door of Jennifer's room. "It's Dan Cameron," he said. "Are you ready?"

"Of course not," she answered waspishly. "None of these damned things fit, and have to be altered."

"My God!" Dan moaned. "It's sundown. You've had two hours already. I'll go find a preacher and fetch him here."

"You'll do nothing of the kind," she said. "Everything's been arranged. The ceremony will be held at the First Baptist Church at eight-thirty, with the Reverend Mr. George Caldwell officiating. Now go away. I've got enough to worry me without you yowling about the time."

"Is there someone in there with you?" Dan demanded.

"Of course," she answered. "One of the ladies was kind enough to offer to help me. That's more than you're doing."

"Come on, big fella," Lennie said, taking Dan's arm and guiding him to the stairs. "Let's eat. I'm starved. She's worth waitin' fer. I used to think that all gals was sugar an' spice, like my mom used to tell me. It ain't true. Some of 'em are. There's others thet ain't."

Dan waited until they had reached the street. "You're thinking of Tansie, aren't you?" he asked slowly. "You don't like your sister-in-law. Why?"

Lennie didn't answer until they had walked some distance from the hotel toward an eating house. "She might be in on it," he finally said.

"In on what?" Dan demanded.

"On what's goin' on," Lennie said doggedly. "In with Bart Webb to run homesteaders out o' the basin."

"These are terrible things you're saying," Dan cautioned. "Tansie was Ed's wife. You don't think she had anything to do with *that*, do you?"

"No," Lennie admitted. "It's only since Ed was killed that she began actin' scared."

"Scared?"

"Like she's afeared of bein' killed like Ed was. Like she knows too much an' wished she didn't."

"About what?"

"About Bart Webb, maybe," Lennie said. "About somethin' big, somethin' Bart Webb knows about."

Dan ran an arm around Lennie's shoulders. "You must be wrong," he said. "Anyway, let's forget about it for tonight at least. You're to be my best man. And I want you to be another pair of eyes for me. Tansie isn't the only one who's scared. I'm scared too. I want to tell you one thing, Lennie. I'm not Bart Webb's man. I'm my own man, with no stake in this, except that you wrote a letter to me asking me to help your brother. That's the only reason I came here."

Lennie leaned against him, fighting back tears. "That's what I wanted to hear," he choked. "I'll help be your eyes."

They entered the eating place. Lennie ate with a healthy appetite, but Dan, for once, could only pick at his food. He watched a rickety hansom cab pass by and pull up in front of the hotel, which was in sight down the street through the restaurant window. The driver alighted, tethered the team to the rail, and entered the hotel. Presently he returned, freed the horses, and mounted the box. He sat waiting.

Jennifer Spring appeared. Dan's breath caught in his throat. She was wearing a white bridal gown and gloves and high-heeled slippers. A filmy veil drifted in the soft, warm night breeze. Accompanying her and assisting her into the shabby cab was Father Terence O'Flaherty.

Dan sat transfixed as the cab got under way, wheeled and

passed by again on its way down the street. He arose from the table.

He walked numbly out of the restaurant with Lennie following. Soft organ music was drifting through the warm night from the Baptist church at the west end of the street. The cab was halting in front of the church. Father O'Flaherty and Jennifer alighted and mounted the steps of the church.

Dan and Lennie walked to the church and entered the vestibule. A small, gentle-faced man in clerical garb, along with a middle-aged woman in a pink dress were waiting, along with Father O'Flaherty.

"I am the Reverend Mr. George Caldwell," the minister said, shaking hands. "This is my wife. The bride has asked her to stand as matron of honor. You, of course, are the bridegroom. Who will stand with you?"

"Me," Lennie said. "What do I do?"

"Just do as I say," the minister said. He lifted a hand. Dan and Lennie followed him to the altar. A woman who sat at a small organ struck up the wedding march.

The door from the vestry opened. Jennifer appeared and placed a hand on Father O'Flaherty's arm. The gown she had found was not silk or satin, but on her it had richness and radiance. The veil was so thin he could see her eyes. They were regarding him soberly, fearlessly.

She moved to his side and he took her hand. He had the unreal sensation of living over the most joyous moment of his life, of standing again with the fingers of a girl resting trustingly in his hand, of hearing the words that pledged love, faith and loyalty until death did them—

He flinched, almost withdrew his hand. But Jennifer Spring's fingers tightened on his palm, holding him there. Her eyes were glistening. She understood his thoughts, knew that he was living again a terrible moment. She knew that he was afraid the story would be repeated. Afraid for her.

He realized that the minister was waiting for an answer. "I do," he mumbled. He heard Jennifer echo the words when the vow was put to her. He found himself slipping on her slender finger the wedding ring that Father O'Flaherty had placed in his hand. He heard the pronouncement: ". . . man and wife."

Jennifer lifted the veil, awaiting the sealing kiss. He bent. Her lips were cold, quivering.

"Bless you, my children," Father O'Flaherty said huskily. "And may God look after you both."

Jennifer linked her arm with his. They started down the aisle. It was then that he discovered that the church was not as entirely empty as it had been when he had arrived. Two persons sat in the rear pew. Bart Webb and his wife. Consuelo wore a finely woven mantilla over her hair and had on a wine-red Spanish gown that was fashioned in an older period—tight-bodied, bare-shouldered. It was a gown for fiestas, for dancing, for weddings. Bart Webb was also garbed in Spanish fashion—bolero jacket, pleated white shirt, velvet breeches slashed at the ankle. Evidently the Webbs had sent to their ranch for the finery.

Dan saw that he was being searched grimly by Bart Webb's steel-gray eyes and was being asked a silent question. Tears stained Consuelo Webb's cheeks. She too was asking a question, but it was of Jennifer Spring that it was being asked. And with great concern.

Dan looked at the girl beside him. Jennifer Spring's lips were parted in a little smile. The smile was intended for Consuelo Webb as though meant to reassure her of something.

Then they were out of the church. The cab was still waiting. Jennifer had arranged everything. A few bystanders had wandered into the vicinity, but Pinedale mainly had retreated back of closed doors—waiting and listening.

CHAPTER NINE

Dan helped Jennifer into the cab. He handed Lennie a gold piece. "Paint the town," he said. "But no booze or women. I'll see you tomorrow."

He climbed into the cab. "I guess you know where to go," he told the driver, who was a Mexican.

The driver grinned. "Sí, señor," he said. Then in perfect English. "I sure do." He cracked the whip, startling his ancient team into a shambling gallop that carried them the few blocks to the hotel.

Several spectators were in the sitting room, pretending to be disinterested, but were, instead, apprehensive and ready to take cover. All Pinedale seemed keyed for trouble, as though fearing a fuse to a bomb was burning.

Dan and Jennifer ascended the stairs and walked to the door of the room she occupied. She produced the key from a small, beaded purse she was carrying and handed it to him. He unlocked the door and stood aside for her to enter.

But she stood there. "You fool!" she breathed. "Carry me over the threshold, as you're supposed to do. People are watching."

Dan discovered that the clerk and as many others from the sitting room as could crowd their way partly up the stairs were gaping. Doors of other guests along the hallway had opened and eyes were peering.

He lifted Jennifer in his arms and carried her into the room, kicking the door emphatically shut. The lamp had been left burning. He set Jennifer on her feet and locked the door.

She straightened her bonnet and brushed at her gown. She removed the veil. She was suddenly subdued and no longer in command of the situation.

Dan peered around the room. There were two windows. The lower sashes had been raised for ventilation, but the shades were tightly drawn. He moved to one, careful not to let his shadow fall on the shade, lifted a corner to give him an eyehole. The window overlooked the flat roof of an adjoining structure that apparently was a carpenter's shop, judging by the clutter of lumber and discarded material at the rear. There was a space of some six feet between the buildings.

He started to remove his coat, then decided that he would be more visible in his white shirt and retained the coat. Jennifer was watching, puzzled and frowning as he crouched, peering and listening.

Deciding that the coast was clear, he blew out the lamp, lifted the shade part way, then thrust a leg over the sill. "What in the world?" Jennifer gasped. "Do you really have to go that far to keep our agreement?"

"Don't jump to conclusions," Dan grunted. "I want to do a little scouting. I'll be back. Light the lamp once I'm on my way."

He lowered himself to arm's length and dropped. The distance was only a few feet and he landed without injury. He crouched there, listening again to make sure his exit from the hotel had gone unnoticed.

He crept to the front corner of the building and peered into the street. Pinedale was quiet, retreating again into its shell. Two or three pedestrians were in sight, but they were a distance away and interested only in whatever was their destination. The billiard room on the opposite side of the street was still lighted and he could hear the click of pool balls.

Dan's objective was Alex Coates's blacksmith shop which stood some two blocks west, beyond the better-lighted area. It was on the same side of the street as the hotel and he retreated, edged his way among the clutter at the rear of the carpenter's shop, and finally brought up at the wagonyard. There was a small cottage at the rear of the yard, whose windows showed light. Dan guessed that this was where Alex Coates lived. If so, the light might mean that he was home.

Then the door of the cottage opened, sending a lance of light across the disorder in the wagonyard. There were voices too far away to be intelligible. Two men left the cottage, walked through the wagonyard and onto the street. Alex Coates and Max Largo. Dan circled the sagging wire fence enclosing the yard and watched the pair walk down the street and enter a saloon.

He moved onto the street and faded through the open wagon gate of the yard. The blacksmith shop stood with closed double doors, but only a worn horseshoe had been used to secure the hasp in place of a padlock.

Dan freed the hasp and moved into the blackness of the shop, which bore the sooty pungency of all shops of its kind. He had only a few matches in his pocket, but he managed to locate a dingy lamp, which he lighted, turning down the wick to give a minimum of light. He peered around. The forge fire was banked but gave forth heat. An anvil dominated the working space. Heavy tools were chained to the walls. A large toolbox built of thick planks stood under a workbench, chained and padlocked.

A clutter of discarded horseshoes and wagon and well-digging equipment lay in a corner. Dan poked among it, but found nothing of interest. He looked longingly at the locked toolbox but had to give up the idea of smashing into it because the noise was sure to betray his presence—and his purpose.

He snuffed the lamp and left the cavelike shop. He paused in the repair yard to listen, and decided it was safe to move into the street. He was wrong.

As he emerged from the wagon gate a big figure loomed in the dim light. Alex Coates! He had been crouching in the shadows, waiting.

"You dirty thief!" Coates rasped. "What were you doin' in my shop?"

"Looking for a horseshoe," Dan said. "A big one."

"I thought so," Coates gritted. "Well, yo're through lookin' —forever. I had a hunch who it was when I saw the light in my shop."

As Coates spoke he was upon Dan with clubbing fists. Dan did not attempt to draw his six-shooter, but only tried to ward off the blows that Coates was driving at his head and body. Above all, he wanted Coates to stay alive and do more talking.

The man was grizzlylike in size and grizzlylike in savage strength. Dan knew he could not stand toe to toe with his opponent. Then he realized that he was fighting for his life, as Coates had said. The blacksmith meant to kill him.

He clinched with the man and called on his body for a supreme burst of strength. He managed to bend, lift Coates's bulk on his shoulder, and toss him over his head. Coates landed heavily on the sunbaked clay of the sidewalk. That slowed him down, but he came to his feet, panting, slobbering frenziedly. He had found a weapon in the shape of a fist-sized rock, which he brought down, intending to smash it on Dan's head. Dan faded aside in time and the rock grazed his shoulder. That gave him a chance to smash a right fist to Coates's jaw and a left to the stomach. Coates shed the blows and managed to grasp Dan's hair. He yanked and Dan felt agony. He drove a knee into Coates's groin. That weakened the man so that he tore free.

They had been carried into the middle of the street by the fury of their battle. Dan was dimly aware that spectators had arrived but were staying at a distance, watching in silence.

He took a smash to the side of the head that sent him reeling, and he fell. Coates leaped high, intending to come down on his stomach with all his weight. He managed to roll aside. He grasped one of Coates's legs and arose, twisting so that Coates was again thrown in a somersault to land flat on

112

his back. Coates tried to get up but sagged back, his strength gone.

The scene was spinning before Dan's eyes. He started toward Alex Coates, the battle lust blazing in his eyes. He was bleeding, caked with blood and dust. Then he felt arms encircle him and heard Jennifer's voice. "No! No!" she screamed. "It's over! Don't kill him!"

The blood that was dripping from his damaged face was staining her wedding dress. He grasped Coates by the hair, shook him bitterly. "Who's paying you?" he gritted. "What's in this for all of you?"

Coates looked at him with glazed eyes. Dan felt that the man was about to answer. Then Coates closed his gashed lips.

Dan released his grip and let Coates slump into the dust. He reeled to his knees. Jennifer tried to help him to his feet but he doggedly pushed her away and rose on his own power.

Sheriff Honeywell arrived, breathless, and pushed through the bystanders. "You?" he exploded, glaring at Dan. "Now what started *this?*"

"I only wanted to ask the price of an oversized horseshoe," Dan mumbled.

Jennifer led him toward the door of the hotel. "You're a fine picture of a bridegroom," she moaned. "Look at your clothes! Ruined!"

Lennie arrived and Jennifer sent him to bring the doctor. "Tell him he's got some bandaging and sewing to do," she said. "This man is a mess."

She marched Dan upstairs to her room. She seated him on a chair, removed the remains of his coat and shirt. Pinning up the sleeves of her wedding gown, she sloshed water from the pitcher into the china basin and began carefully washing away the blood and dust on his face.

The doctor arrived after a time and took over. "Sorry I couldn't make it sooner," he said. "I had to do some patch-ing on Alex Coates. He was in worse shape than this one. Much worse."

He finished the stitching and court plastering. "No busted bones as far as I can find out," he said. "But you'll bear scars. That'll be a dollar and a half."

Dan surveyed himself in the dresser mirror. An eye was swelling shut, and each time he moved his jaw pain darted through him. But he had fared better than he had feared.

Jennifer paid the doctor with money from her purse. She pushed both Lennie and the doctor out of the room and closed the door.

"Let's place our cards on the table," she said. "Do you still think Bart Webb is the man back of all this deviltry?"

"Everybody seems to think so," Dan said.

"But what do *you* think?" she demanded.

Before Dan could frame an answer, a gunshot sounded somewhere in the town. The heavy report echoed against walls. For a space there was dead silence in the street. Dan had the impression that Pinedale was once more freezing—waiting, listening in fear.

A man's voice lifted in the distance. "My God! Git Honeywell, somebody. We got another murder! It's Alex Coates! Looks like he's daid."

Dan left the room, followed by Jennifer. They raced down the hall to the front of the building, where a screen door opened onto a covered gallery which overlooked the street. It had rocking chairs and benches for guests on hot evenings.

The big, square figure of Bart Webb was on the sidewalk directly across the street. He was peering eastward where activity was boiling up. Dan had the impression that the rancher had been strolling westward when the shot had sounded.

Down the street a voice arose, dominating the growing hubbub. "How long are we goin' to stand for these murders? We all know who brung that gunman from Wyomin' to do his dirty work. What both of them need is a taste of the rope. If

114

we got any guts it's time we did some stringin' up, startin' with Bart Webb an' his killer."

The speaker was Abel Jenkins. Another voice loudly backed Jenkins' demand. That speaker was Jenkins' shadow, Pete Slater. "Find 'em an' lynch 'em!" Slater bellowed. "Let's git rid of this range hawg an' his outfit, once an' fer all!"

The majority of the listeners milled about uncertainly, but young boys were arriving and taking up the shout, thirsty for any kind of excitement.

The sheriff and his deputy arrived and moved into the center of the group. "That'll do with that kind of talk," the officer bellowed. "I'll take charge here."

The bystanders fell back, but the spark had been applied and they were being harangued by Abel Jenkins and Slater. Dan was aware of a growing sullen fury. Eventually Slater and Jenkins moved away, taking with them the noisiest segment of the throng.

"Go home, all of you!" Honeywell yelled at them. "Or I'll run you in."

"Seems like Bart Webb an' that Wyomin' gunslinger ought to be the ones you run in, Jim," Jenkins shouted back.

"I'll decide that," Honeywell boomed. "You there, Sam Summers, git a stretcher. Whar's Doc Berrington? Looks like Alex is dead, but we got to have it official."

The doctor arrived and examined the huddled body that still lay on the sidewalk. Presently a stretcher was brought and Alex Coates's body was carried to the furniture store. The sheriff and his deputy came striding determinedly toward the hotel.

"Looks like I'm likely to be arrested," Dan said to Jennifer.

"Luckily you have me as an alibi," she said.

"If they'll believe it again," Dan said dubiously.

CHAPTER TEN

Jim Honeywell didn't know what to believe. He stood in the room, red-faced, angry, but balked, glaring from Dan to Jennifer. "Alibi, alibi!" he raged. "This is the third time, an' I've had about enough of it. First it was Clem Coates up in Rimrock, then it was her backin' yore stoiy when Cal Seal-over was killed. Now, here it is agin. Hand over yore gun, Cameron."

Dan passed over the weapon. Honeywell flipped open the cylinder and dropped the shells into the palm of his left hand. He inspected them and scowled, frustrated. "Still four live ones," he admitted. "What do you think, Bill?"

His deputy inspected the gun, held the barrel to the light, and sniffed at the muzzle. "Ain't been fired lately," he said, shrugging. "Ain't been cleaned since he touched off that one he admitted shootin' at Cal Sealover the other night. No fresh powder smoke."

"What kind of a gun was Coates killed with?" Dan asked. "Where did the shot come from?"

"Six-gun from the sound an' the look of the wound," Honeywell said. "Won't know fer sure till the doc makes his autopsy. Seems like somebody staked out between buildin's across the street from the Golden Lion an' blasted Alex down with one slug. Nobody actually seen it as fur as I know. I've just started investigatin'."

"I take it that you suspect Bart Webb?" Jennifer demanded.

"I ain't sayin'," Honeywell said wearily. "But he better have one of them alibis you two are so good at."

"I saw Bart Webb right across the street from this hotel within seconds after the shot was fired," Dan said. "So did Miss—my wife. He couldn't possibly have killed Coates."

"I might have knowed," Honeywell sighed. "You two air good at alibis fer yoreselves, but I never figgered you'd be helpin' out Bart Webb."

An ominous sound was rising from the town. It was the confused shouting of men. Honeywell listened to it for a moment. "Lynch mob!" he snapped. "I'm puttin' you two in the calaboose—for safekeepin' if nothin' else. You know what that screechin' means, Cameron. I happen to know you've heard it a time or two in the past. They're after you, an' they're after Bart Webb. I'll jug him too if I can locate him."

"Give us time to at least change out of these clothes," Jennifer protested.

"Bring yore duds with you," Honeywell answered. "Change in the jail. You ain't got much time as it is, if what I hear means anythin'."

Lennie appeared. "You sure are dumb, sheriff," he raged.

Ignoring the youth, Honeywell let them gather spare clothing, then marched them out of the hotel, where he turned them over to Bill Royce. The deputy hustled them down a side street to the sheriff's office. Lennie followed at their heels but Royce refused to permit him to enter the building.

Dan and Jennifer were led to the small dingy cell room at the rear, which contained eight cages. He started to lock them in the same cell.

"Separate cells, you fool!" Jennifer exclaimed. "Don't you have any sense of decency?"

"But you two air married!" Royce protested.

"I don't care to debate it with you," she snapped. "I have to change clothes and don't care to be locked up with Mr. Cameron."

Royce, dumbfounded, locked them in cells as far apart as possible and went away grumbling. Dan listened to the shouting. It was growing in volume and moving nearer.

Voices sounded in the office. Honeywell was talking. "I got no time to argue with you now. Lock 'em up, Bill. We're in fer real trouble."

Bill Royce returned to the cell room, leading Bart Webb and his wife. Consuelo was pushed into a cell next to Jennifer's cage and Bart Webb into one alongside Dan's place.

"There hasn't been a Valdez in jail since my father was arrested for hanging a cattle thief," Consuelo spoke. "He was acquitted."

Bart Webb laughed. "You're keeping up the family tradition, *querida*," he said.

"At least we have company in misery," Consuelo Webb said. "It *is* Mr. Cameron, isn't it?"

"It is," Dan said.

"Where is Miss—your wife, Señor Cameron?" she asked.

"Present," Jennifer spoke from the far cell. "So you are under arrest also, Señora Webb. Do they suspect you also of killing the blacksmith?"

"Apparently so," Consuelo Webb sighed. "But I do have witnesses to prove that I was elsewhere when the shot was fired. We are staying at the home of our old friends, Joe Tracy, the barber, and his wife, Mary. I was there. Not so my poor husband. He was alone in the town at the time."

"It happens that we can testify that he, at least, did not fire the shot," Dan said. "Miss Spring can corroborate that."

"My name," Jennifer spoke from the gloom, "is now Mrs. Daniel Cameron. You may as well get used to it, Mr. Cameron."

"I just can't believe it," Consuelo Webb said. "I—"

They dropped that line of discussion and listened to the approaching roar of the mob. Honeywell came hurrying into the cell room. He had belted on a brace of pistols. Royce was with him, carrying a buckshot gun, broken for safety at the moment, revealing its wicked double load of brass-rimmed shells.

"There's only me an' Bill," Honeywell said. "We might be able to bluff 'em off, but four of us would be better than two—'specially if one of us was Dan Cameron. We don't cotton to maybe have to shoot fellers that have been friends an' neighbors, 'specially some of them young squirts what are in this jest fer the hell of it."

"So?" Dan asked.

"So, what if you an' Mr. Webb here, stood up for yore-selves alongside me'n Bill an' cooled 'em down? We're bein' paid fer things like this, but you two has got a little more at stake. These fellers out there mean business right now."

"What do you want us to do?" Bart Webb demanded. "Go out there and tell them to go away? I haven't got a toothpick on me to bluff 'em with. You took my gun."

"I'll give you yore guns," Honeywell said. "But, on one promise. There's to be no shootin' unless I give the word. That'll be only as a last resort."

He looked at Dan. "I understood you faced down a lynch mob a time or two in yore days in northern country," he said. "I reckon I ain't that caliber. I'm skeered. I got a wife an' two kids. I'd like to live through this night."

Dan became sure of one thing. Jim Honeywell, at least, was honest and conscientious. "There'll be no need for killing if this is handled right, Sheriff," he said. "It sounds like a small bunch and half of them are likely crazy, brainless kids. That's usually the way it is. They're being pushed into it."

"What are you driving at?" Honeywell demanded.

"Somebody's prodding them, most likely," Dan said. "The thing is to find out who's making the most noise and is standing back of the ones they're shoving into the front ranks. That's generally the way with lynch mobs. Now let's go out there. They're coming on the run."

"Give me a gun, Jim Honeywell!" Consuelo Webb demanded. "I am going out there too. Do you think I intend to stay cooped up here and be at the mercy of those fools if they get past you men?"

"I can't do that, Consuelo," Honeywell said as he released Dan and Bart Webb from their cells. "I'll open yore cells also, but you ladies must stay here. Come on, Bart! An' you too, Cameron!"

They rushed into the office, where the sheriff handed Dan and Bart Webb their pistols. Bill Royce was loading rifles and replacing them in a wall case that was unlocked.

The tumult reached the jail. "Come out, Honeywell!" a voice screeched. "We got no quarrel with you, but we're fed up on you lettin' killers walk around loose when we all know who they are! It's Bart Webb we want! Him an' thet hired killer he brung in from Wyomin' to help with his dirty work!"

Honeywell started to shout a refusal, but Dan silenced him with a gesture. "Unlock the door," he said.

"You goin' out there?" the sheriff croaked.

"And you with me, and Webb and Royce too," Dan said. "Make 'em fight or quit."

He unlocked the door himself and walked out onto the small platform that fronted the building. Honeywell moved with him and stood shoulder to shoulder. Bart Webb joined them and then Bill Royce. They were all big men, grim, armed. They held their six-shooters cocked but dangling downward. The shotgun in Bill Royce's arms was still open so that the shells in the barrels could be seen.

They stood facing a score of opponents. Several were teenage boys. A few were obviously whiskey-soaked barflies, men who could be drafted into any cause for the price of a few drinks. Only a few seemed to be ranchers or settlers from claims and outfits that Lennie had said were still active in pockets along the bluffs overlooking the basin.

The ringleader was Abel Jenkins. He stood well in the rear, carrying a coil of rope over his shoulder which had the traditional hangman's noose, held by thirteen twists. With him was Pete Slater, who was carrying a brace of pistols in his hands.

The howling faded uncertainly. Abel Jenkins tried to rise to the occasion. "Don't be bluffed, boys!" he screeched. "They won't shoot. Stand aside, Jim Honeywell, or take the consequences."

Two more persons stepped out of the jail office and joined the four men on the platform. They were Consuelo Webb, who moved to the side of her husband, and Jennifer, who took her place with Dan. They carried rifles they had taken from the case in the sheriff's office.

Then Lennie came out of hiding at the corner of the building and leaped to the platform to stand with them. He had a six-shooter in his hand.

That silenced Jenkins, but only for a moment. "You mean you'd stoop to hidin' back of petticoats, Jim?" he croaked. But he had lost and knew it. The mob spirit, easily fanned to a flame, had died as quickly.

Jenkins, trying to salvage what he could out of his defeat, turned his wrath on Dan. "I've heard that you had a yalla streak up yore back, Cameron. A big reputation, a big bluff. You was hell on drunks an' greenhorns when you wore the badge, but you never faced up to a real man in yore life. You hid back of a woman once before an' she got killed. Now yo're hidin' behind petticoats agin."

Dan left the line, descending the steps to the sidewalk. Jennifer tried to stop him, but he refused and her hand fell away.

"We'll try it out, Jenkins," Dan said. "You back off a dozen paces. You and your heel dog with you. I'll do the same. Both of you can draw any time you like. Now, if you want. You could hardly miss at this range."

There was a rush to move out of line. Abel Jenkins edged back a pace. He threw the hangrope into the dust. Pete Slater did not move. "No you don't!" Jenkins squealed. "I wouldn't have a chance, an' you know it. You're a gunfighter, an' I'm just an honest, peace-lovin' citizen. You'd like to add another notch to your score, wouldn't you? But I ain't fallin' for it."

Dan looked at Pete Slater. "How about you?" he asked. The hard-eyed man did not answer. Jenkins turned on his heel and walked away, and Slater followed him.

Willis Mason and Max Largo had appeared in the background, and had been listening and watching. Mason now came hurrying through the scattering mob, which was a mob no longer.

"Good work, Jim!" he exclaimed. "And my congratulations to you, Bart, and to you, Consuelo. You both were magnificent." He added, soberly, "But I'm afraid it's time to quit, Bart. Life is being made miserable for you. I happen to know that Abel Jenkins is trying to buy the Circle W. Maybe that's the best way out."

"Consuelo's kin, and mine, are buried in the ranch graveyard," Bart Webb said. "We would never turn that ground over to a stranger, let alone to a man like Abel Jenkins."

"I'll tell you what I'll do, Bart," Mason said. "I'll pay you a fair price for the ranch. I'll match Jenkins' offer and a little more. Then, after all this blows over, if you and Consuelo ever decide you want to come back, I'll sell it back to you. How's that for settling everything?"

Consuelo spoke. "No! No, Mr. Mason. We will not be driven from our home by evil persons." She turned to the sheriff. "Are we still under arrest, Mr. Honeywell?"

"Course not," Honeywell said. "All I ask is that the pack of you git out of town." He glared at Dan and Jennifer. "An' if I never see either of you ag'in it would add years to my life."

Dan nodded and offered his arm to Jennifer. "We will now continue our interrupted honeymoon."

They parted from the Webbs and headed toward the Pioneer Hotel. Lennie started to follow them, but Consuelo seized him by the coattail. "It would be better if you came with us," she said. "We are staying at the Tracy home. Maybe Mary Tracy will make popcorn and fudge and lemonade. We will all be merry and toast the bridal couple."

Lennie pulled free, flushing. "I'll take care of myself," he blurted out and went hurrying away, but not toward the hotel. "I kin take a hint."

It was evident to Dan that Lennie still was wary of Bart Webb.

CHAPTER ELEVEN

Jennifer was trembling a little and trying not to show it as she and Dan entered her room at the Pioneer. She removed her bonnet and was pretending to be very busy at the dresser mirror arranging her hair when she discovered that, once more, Dan was thrusting a leg over the sill of the open window, preparing to make an exit.

"Oh, for heaven's sake!" she exclaimed. "Have you gone entirely loco?"

"Maybe," Dan said. "I still want to find what I was looking for the first time. I'll be back."

"And what are you looking for?" she demanded. "You came back the other time all right, but almost on a stretcher. Are you trying for more bandages?"

Dan dropped to the ground, ending the conversation. Jennifer's head jutted from the window, but he made a gesture, shushing her into silence. Waiting his chance, he once more made his way to Alex Coates's blacksmith shop. He lighted the sooty lamp. Locating a length of iron, he used it to pry off the hasp of the padlock that secured the heavy lid of the toolbox. Delving into the box he located among the tools a grimy canvas saddlebag. It contained a large horseshoe—the largest Dan had ever seen. Forged to its inner surface was a bar to which was also forged a threaded sleeve of a common water pipe. Delving into the box again he found a short length of threaded water pipe. He knew that with this fitted into the sleeve, a man on horseback, or on foot, could forge false prints of the great shoe in dust or soft ground.

He did not need the length of pipe, but carried the shoe in the canvas bag as he left the blacksmith yard unseen and made his way back to the hotel. He walked swiftly past the drowsy desk clerk and up the stairs, holding the pouch out of sight. He tapped on the door of the room and said, "It's Cameron, Mrs. Cameron."

Jennifer came with a rush to admit him. "What's that?" she demanded with distaste as he placed the grimy pouch on the nightstand. "It looks filthy."

"It's one of the reasons why Alex Coates was murdered," he said. "Are you packed?"

"Packed? Where are we going?"

"Back to the Vickers claim. At least you'll have a roof over your head there. We're newlyweds, you know. Maybe it's time we began acting the part."

She eyed him. "Just how far does this acting go?" she demanded.

"I'll stay in my place, if you'll stay in yours," Dan said.

She uttered a sniff and began hurriedly placing her belongings in a case. "I wouldn't trust any man, least of all you, as far as I could throw a steer by the tail," she said.

Lennie was waiting in the lobby for instructions. "You bring my roan out to the claim tomorrow," Dan told him. "We'll go out there in the wagon tonight."

He and Jennifer hurried to the livery and awakened the night hostler, and Dan sped the task of hitching Jennifer's team to her wagon. He hid the weighted saddlebag among the trunks and hatboxes that littered the wagon. "Great guns!" he exclaimed. "You must have tried to buy out the mercantile. I'd hate to be your husband for real. You better look around for a millionaire."

She ignored that and started to take over the driver's side of the seat, and was about to pick up the reins when Dan mounted into the wagon, crowded her over, and took the lines from her hands.

"I still don't hanker to wind up in a gully with a wagon on top of me," he said.

She ignored that also. She remained silent for the first mile or more of the ride through the pines into the rolling, open basin. The hour was nearing midnight when Dan heard an oncoming vehicle approaching, with a team at a fast trot. The trail was so narrow at that point that the driver was forced to lean back on the reins and use the brake when they met in the moonlight. The vehicle was Tansie's covered wagon. She sat alone on the seat.

Dan leaped to the ground and seized the bridle of the near horse as she attempted to crowd the team and wagon past. "Tansie?" he exclaimed. "Where are you going?"

"Get out of the way, Dan!" Tansie replied, her voice high-pitched. "I'm—I'm leaving."

"You mean now—tonight? Why?"

"I don't want to be killed!" she sobbed. "They think I know the secret."

"The secret? What secret? And who are *they*?"

She lifted the whip to lash the horses into motion. Dan seized her arm, blocking the attempt. "Calm down, Tansie!" he said. "It's time to talk."

"I've said too much already!" Tansie wept. "Let me go, Dan! Please let me go!"

Jennifer spoke. "It's more than time to talk, Tansie. I want to know several things. Why did you put that knife in my pillow at Rimrock that night? And set fire to my wagon on the trail? Now don't deny it. That perfume you use was in the air in my room that night. And when the fire started under my wagon I could see the curtain still swaying on your wagon after you had rushed back there to hide."

Dan peered at Jennifer. "You didn't happen to mention these things to me," he said. "Why?"

"I have my reasons," she answered. "Tansie, why did you try to kill me?"

127

"I didn't, I didn't!" Tansie wailed. "I only tried to scare you. They made me do it."

"Who?"

"I don't know," Tansie wept. "I found a note in my room telling me what to do. It said I would be killed if I didn't. It said you came here only to make trouble and that you must be scared into leaving."

"Keep talking, Tansie," Jennifer said relentlessly. "You may even know who killed your husband."

"Dear God, no!" Tansie said.

"Who was it?" Jennifer insisted.

"I think it was Alex Coates," she sobbed.

Dan spoke. "Alex Coates was killed from ambush tonight. Do you know why?"

"Ed had stumbled on the secret of where the treasure was buried," Tansie said. "Alex Coates had found it. It must have been somewhere around the old mission—Santa Rosalia. That's where the treasure is supposed to have been buried. Clem, his brother, must have known the secret also. Now they are both dead—murdered. Like Ed. Like everybody who has had anything to do with Bart Webb in the basin."

Dan felt his flesh prickle. He and Jennifer had broken into hideous secrets. "Do you realize what you're saying, Tansie?" he asked hoarsely. "Just what is this treasure?"

It was Jennifer who answered that. "It's an old legend. It's called the treasure of Santa Rosalia. It is supposed to be worth millions."

Once more Dan was struck by the realization that Jennifer knew much about this area. "Millions?" he said incredulously. "That's hard to believe."

"What else would drive men to commit the crimes that are already done?" Tansie wept. "Murder, terror, settlers driven out under threat of death."

"How did Ed find out the Coates brothers had located this treasure?" Dan asked. "And what did they do with it?"

"I don't know," Tansie said. "Ed's letter said that he

happened to hear the Coates brothers talking when they were drunk. He had gone to the blacksmith shop after dark to get a wagon bolt made to replace one that had broken in our wagon on the trail outside of town. He heard enough to know they had found it. They must have seen him leaving, or heard him and guessed that he knew too much. That was why he was murdered."

"You mentioned a letter," Dan said. "What letter?"

"It was one Ed wrote to you, Dan, after he got back from town that night. It told about finding a clue to the treasure and asked you to come and help him."

"I never got the letter," Dan said.

"I never mailed it," Tansie said. "I didn't see any point in getting you involved. I hid it under a false bottom in the top drawer of my dresser. You can find it there. Now let me go. I want to make it to Rimrock, sell the team and wagon, and take the stage out. I've got folks in Nebraska."

Dan saw that it was hopeless to try to detain her. He released his grip on her arm and stood aside. Tansie used the whip on the team and the wagon lurched away.

"You'll never live to leave this basin unless you do what I'm doing, Dan," she called back. The wagon vanished into the shadows of the timber up the trail to Pinedale.

"I feel sorry for her," Dan said to Jennifer.

"She's a mercenary woman," Jennifer said grimly. "At first she decided to try to find that treasure for herself. That's why she never mailed that letter to you. She thinks Alex Coates murdered her husband, but she didn't turn a hand to help another man when he was being tried for a crime she feels that Coates committed."

"You mean Bart Webb, of course," Dan said. "I think she's right about Alex Coates having bushwhacked Ed. He planted those big hoofprints with that special shoe he made at his shop to incriminate Bart Webb. He must have been the one who was with Cal Sealover the night they shot up our beds. He either didn't want to leave Sealover there wounded so

129

that he might talk, or he probably had orders in the first place to see to it that Sealover didn't stay alive in any event. He planted those shoe prints the next morning. He was the last one to show up while the sheriff was palavering with us over Sealover's body."

"What about Clem Coates?" Jennifer chattered. "The pitchfork?"

"My guess is that Abel Jenkins did that," Dan said. "The chances were that all those hard feelings they pretended on the stage trip was faked to cover up the fact they were in cahoots as far as the treasure was concerned. You upset that for them when you pushed Clem into the gully. Then Abel Jenkins decided to put Clem out of the way for good and try to put the blame on me. Either that or he had orders to do it."

"And Sealover?"

"He seems to have been a cheap hoodlum. I think he was hired to pose as a nester and told to lean on Bart Webb that day. He didn't know he was being set up himself to be rubbed out."

"Do you still believe it was Bart Webb who is giving the orders and doing the setting up?" Jennifer demanded.

"I never said I believed anything either way," Dan replied.

"You're as stupid as Cal Sealover was," she snapped.

"Maybe so, but I think Tansie isn't the only one who didn't tell everything she knows."

"Meaning that you suspect I'm here for the same thing," she cried. "You think I'm here to get my hands on the blasted treasure."

Before Dan could answer, she climbed into the wagon and picked up the reins. "Hike!" she shouted. The horses leaped ahead.

Dan, taken by surprise, managed to grab the tailgate as the wagon lurched ahead, and hauled himself aboard. He scrambled through the wagon to the seat, and took over control of the horses.

"You seem to be in the habit of leaving men afoot," he said.

"If things like that got out there'd be talk. I'm supposed to be your husband, remember?"

"Also remember that we have an agreement," she said. "We can begin keeping it by giving me more room on the seat of this wagon. Your responsibility is nothing more than as a bodyguard. Otherwise stay as far away from me as possible."

"Glad to accommodate," Dan said, inching away. "I'd as soon cozy up to a bobcat."

They drove in silence until the ridgepole of the house Tansie had abandoned loomed off the trail. Dan swung the team onto the wagon road leading to the house, which stood black and unlighted. He halted the horse, wrapped the reins around the stock, and alighted.

He looked up at Jennifer, who still sat on the seat. "Coming?" he asked.

"I don't imagine you'd want another mercenary woman in on the secret," she said.

"If that's what you are, then stay there," Dan said and turned to walk toward the steps to the house.

She scrambled from the wagon and followed close at his heels. "You heartless man, you know I wouldn't think of sitting out there alone in the dark," she chattered.

Dan led the way into the house, fumbled for his matches, and located a lamp. The sitting room showed the signs of Tansie's hurried packing. The bedroom was more of a shambles, with abandoned clothing scattered over the floor.

The drawers of the dresser had been yanked out and overturned, spilling what Tansie had left of their contents on the carpet. A thin square of wood lay alongside one of the drawers. Beyond a doubt it had been the false bottom that Tansie had mentioned. There was no letter.

Dan looked up at Jennifer. "Somebody got here before we did," he said slowly. "And not too long ago. They likely were watching Tansie, and maybe she got that letter out, then decided to leave it there."

131

She crouched closer to him, shivering with fright. "Who?" she quavered.

"Bart Webb, maybe."

He felt her stiffen. "Why are you so determined to accuse him?" she demanded.

"Everybody thinks he's the one."

"Not everybody," she said. "People are like sheep. They run in one direction, then another, wherever barking dogs want them to go. I understand that, for one, Willis Mason doesn't believe Bart Webb is guilty."

"Nor you," Dan said. "Why are you so sure?"

She would not answer that. She looked around, still shaking with fear. "Let's get out of here!" she exclaimed.

"Whoever it was won't be back," Dan said. "He got what he wanted—if there ever was a letter. Tansie might have been stringing us. She might have made up the whole thing."

"Not her," Jennifer said. "She wouldn't have imagination enough. Do you mean you intend to stay here—in this house—tonight?"

"It'll be daybreak in a couple of hours," Dan said. "It's time to get a little sleep. And my stomach tells me I could stand a little grub."

"Your stomach? At a time like this?"

"I get hungry regularly, seems like," Dan said. "It's a habit I've had all my life. I can't sleep when I'm starving."

"Starving? Of all things! Well, I never!"

But she had quit shivering, finding reassurance and strength in his attitude. She no longer darted frightened glances at the outer darkness that was framed by the windows. Tansie had left cold food and bread in the pantry. They munched in silence while coffee was being brought to a boil on the woodstove.

"That ought to carry me to breakfast time at least," Dan said, yawning. "I'll be turning in now."

An awkward pause came. Jennifer bustled around, trying to cover her confusion by clearing up the dishes.

132

"I'll Siwash outside," Dan burst out. He hadn't meant to shout like that.

"Siwash?" Jennifer echoed. "What's that?"

"A Siwash is when you sleep with a rock for a pillow and your belly—stomach—for a blanket," Dan said. "It's north range lingo. I'll be comfortable. Done it lots of times."

"Oh no you don't," she chattered. "I couldn't sleep a wink unless I knew you were close by. You're supposed to be my bodyguard. You can do your Siwashing right in front of the door to the bunkhouse. I'll bunk there after I make sure nobody is hiding under it. The bunkhouse has only one door, at least, and I'll hang something over the windows. Furthermore . . ."

She paused and both of them listened to the creak of wheels and thud of hoofs approaching. Dan drew his pistol and moved to the lamp. He was about to douse the flame when a voice hailed the house. "'Tis a little late to be arrivin', but I'm prayin' you can find sleepin' room for two weary travelers!"

The speaker was Father Terence O'Flaherty. Jennifer uttered a little scream of delight at having her problem solved and rushed to the door. "Oh, Father, I'm so glad!" she exclaimed. "Who's with you? Why it's . . . !"

Once more her voice trailed off. Dan joined her on the small porch. The companion Father O'Flaherty was helping down from his sheep wagon was Consuelo Webb.

The handsome, dark-eyed woman was still wearing the Spanish costume she had donned to witness the wedding. She mounted the steps to the porch, where Dan and Jennifer stood gaping in amazement.

"How are you, my dear?" Consuelo Webb said calmly and placed both hands on Jennifer's cheeks and kissed her affectionately. "I hope I'm not intruding."

Jennifer began to laugh, almost hysterically. "Intruding?" she said. "Of course not."

There was a twinkle in Consuelo's dark eyes as she looked at Dan. "I trust I'm welcome?" she asked.

Dan tried to think of something to say, but could only mumble unintelligibly. Father O'Flaherty spoke from where he was still holding his mules. "I could stand a little help with these long-eared jackrabbits, young man," he said. "Sure an' I'm not as lively as I was twenty years ago, 'specially at three in the mornin'."

Dan numbly stumbled down the steps and helped lead the rig to the small corral and shed, where he stripped off the harness and found water and hay for the mules.

"You two can put up in the bunkhouse," Consuelo Webb called from the house. "Jennifer and I will make out in Tansie's room."

Father O'Flaherty was already heading for the bunkhouse. He had matches, located the lamp, and lighted it. "Sure an' I will sleep like a bear in winter," he said. "I see there is but one bunk and not too big a one at that. I fear—"

"It's yours," Dan said hastily. "I'll make out on the dog-trot. It's a warm night." He saw a twinkle in the padre's eyes that matched the one he had detected in Consuelo Webb.

"This was a put-up job," he said.

"Now why would you say a thing like that, laddie?" the padre asked blandly.

Dan listened to the faint voices from the house. Evidently Consuelo Webb and Jennifer Spring had much to discuss. "It did solve a ticklish situation," he admitted. "You know we're not really married, don't you, Father? And so does Mrs. Webb."

"I am going to bed," the padre said, yawning.

"Whose idea was this?" Dan demanded. "Why did both of you, especially Mrs. Webb, go so far out of your way to follow us here?"

"Good night, young man," the padre said, and he would talk no more.

Dan found his bedding and stretched out on the plank

floor of the dogtrot. The window of the bedroom of the house was nearby and open. Even though it had been a long stretch since he had known a full night's rest he remained awake. Presently Jennifer spoke softly from the dark interior of the house. "Are you there, Dan Cameron?"

"I'm here," Dan murmured. She said nothing more. Presently he heard her soft breathing join that of Consuelo Webb in sleep. Then he dropped asleep also.

It was nearly noon when he fully awakened. Father O'Flaherty was beginning to stir and mumble also. The fragrance of coffee and frying smokemeat came from the kitchen. He dressed in the bunkhouse, doused his head in the washtrough, and said, "Good morning, Father," to the padre, who appeared, complaining of his rheumatism.

Entering the kitchen he found Consuelo, wearing one of Jennifer's gingham aprons, busy at the cookstove. Jennifer had brought some of her luggage and stock of food from her wagon. She wore a white cotton waist and a plain linen skirt and had a scarf around her coppery hair. She and Consuelo Webb seemed to have reached some sort of a close understanding that puzzled Dan.

They ate at the oilcloth-covered table. Father O'Flaherty pronounced the blessing. ". . . And preserve us from the wrath of violent men and from all the dangers of avarice and the lust for unearned wealth . . ." he intoned.

Dan felt that these words were aimed at himself. The padre was undoubtedly referring to the legend of the lost treasure. He brought up the subject after the meal was finished while he and the padre were at the corral, caring for the stock.

"You seem to think there might be something in this story of buried treasure, Father," he said.

The padre shrugged. "You refer to the treasure of Santa Rosalia," he said. "There could be some substance to it. The archives of the mission fathers have recorded as a fact that a foreign ship was wrecked on the California coast some seventy years ago. That was a time of turmoil, of Indian uprisings, and of Mexico driving out their Spanish rulers. The ship was in effect a pirate craft, manned by freebooters who had seized it at an island called Zanzibar off the east coast of Africa. They were cutthroats. They had sacked temples and villages in their part of the world, and managed to get their loot ashore when they were wrecked. They ransacked two of our missions in California, making off with priceless religious relics. They headed eastward into the mountains and were never heard of again by white men. But the Indians have a story that a savage band of strange men, black, brown, and white, pillaged the mission Santa Rosalia, murdered everyone there, and committed such other acts of cruelty that the tribes rose up and destroyed them to the last man."

"And the treasure?" Dan asked.

"Ah, that is the question. The Indians do not want to talk about it, but I have been told by old ones that the pirates were besieged for many days before they were wiped out. Everyone believes they must have buried their loot there. The poor old mission has been ransacked by treasure hunters over the years, but nothing has been found. However, men still search for it."

"And kill for it," Dan said.

The padre eyed him. "What are you trying to say, my son?"

"Someone knows where it is and is out to have it," Dan said slowly. "Someone without conscience or pity."

"Such as Bart Webb?" the padre asked.

"You are asking that question, not me," Dan said.

"You are blind, are you not?" the padre snorted pityingly. "Haven't you realized that the lass who went through that impious marriage rite with you is a Webb herself?"

"What? Say that again!"

"The girl you know as Jennifer Spring is in reality Jennifer Webb, niece of Consuelo and Bart Webb. Why else would the *señora* hover over her to protect her from the evil designs of men such as you may have on her?"

136

CHAPTER TWELVE

Dan was flabbergasted. "I don't savvy . . ." he mumbled. "Why—?"

"She is the daughter of Bart Webb's brother, Anton. He was originally with Bart Webb as a young cowboy at the Circle W. Anton Webb met and married a young Texas girl who was a girlhood friend of Consuelo Webb. Jennifer was born of that marriage in Texas, where Anton Webb managed a sizable ranch owned by his wife's parents. He became very well-to-do, but was killed when Jennifer was nine in a stampede. Jennifer and her mother had visited Bart and Consuelo Webb here in Eagle Basin often, but after Anton Webb's death her mother sold the ranch in Texas and moved east. She sent Jennifer to schools there and in Europe. Jennifer had not seen Eagle Basin in nearly a dozen years. She had been a child the last time, she is now grown up."

"Why did she come back now?" Dan asked numbly.

"She learned through a friend about the trouble the Webbs were in and that her uncle was being tried for murder. She arrived, as you know, the day Bart Webb was freed of that charge, and decided to pose as a settler and try to find out who wants to ruin her uncle. Her mother is an invalid, so she came alone."

"This friend who sent for her was the Reverend Mr. Terence O'Flaherty, I take it," Dan said. "That's why you were on the stagecoach that day. You met her when she got off the train."

"Perhaps," the padre admitted.

"If Bart Webb isn't back of what's going on, then who is?" Dan demanded. "Is it Abel Jenkins?"

"Neither of us can really believe that little, squashy scut as being smart enough to plan the things that are being done, nor to have the money to pay for killers, then to have them silenced."

"That's the way I look at it," Dan said. "But Jenkins is mixed up in it. It's my belief he's the one who drove that pitchfork into Clem Coates that night in Rimrock. Maybe to square up for the way Coates manhandled him on the stage. But maybe to silence him about something else. Jenkins is a rat, but he's a small rat. There's a bigger rat somewhere."

Jennifer appeared from the kitchen door, wearing an apron. "Come and have a touch of wild plum squeeze," she called. "I found a jar of juice that Tansie had put up, and the well water is cold."

"Thanks, Mrs. Cameron," Dan said. "Or would you prefer to be known from now on as Miss Webb?"

Her hands dropped to her sides. She gave the padre a glare. "So you had to blab it, Father," she said.

"And high time," the padre answered.

She looked at Dan. "Does this change anything?"

"Only to confirm my first opinion that you were up to something and sailing under false colors," Dan said. "I would like to ask one question. Was this marriage really necessary?"

"It seemed like a good idea at the time," she said. "I was frightened. In fact, I still am. But it wasn't fair to you. I'm sorry. I hope you'll forgive me. It's over with now, of course. I free you of any obligations—as a bodyguard and everything else."

"Just like that," Dan said.

She nodded. She was losing color. Her lips looked wan. "Just like that," she said. "I've told you I'm sorry. What else can I say?"

Through the window Dan saw Lennie riding down the

trail, heading for the house mounted on the roan. He walked out to meet the youth. "Good boy," he said. "Just in time."

"For what?"

"To look after the ladies for a while. The padre and me are going out to scout around. I've never been to the mission. I'm curious about it."

Lennie shrugged. "You'll find nothing there. It's been combed by plenty of people, includin' Ed. An' me."

"Did it ever occur to you that Ed was killed because he had stumbled onto something that might lead to the treasure?" Dan asked.

Lennie was shaken. "He'd never have kept that from me," he said. "Him an' me was mighty close."

"Yes. But he didn't have time. He had come upon this the night before he was killed."

"How do you know this?"

"I'll tell you when the time comes," Dan said. He had learned what he wanted to know. Tansie had kept whatever Ed had written in the letter from Lennie. "I really don't expect to find the treasure today," he added gently. "I just have a hunch about something."

Father O'Flaherty objected to such exertion on a hot afternoon, but he finally agreed to accompany Dan. All in all the sun was well on its way to the horizon before they mounted to the box of the sheep wagon, which the padre insisted on using for the sake of the comfort of his armchair.

The distance was some three miles, which was nearly an hour's drive at the plodding pace of the mules. Lennie, still disgruntled at his assignment, stood with Consuelo and Jennifer on the porch watching as they drove away.

The house dwindled to doll size in the sweep of the rolling basin in back of them. The house kept disappearing and reappearing as the sheep wagon creaked over the swells in the land. The warm wind brought the fresh smell of water and willows from the brushy river bottom which paralleled the trail to their right.

They topped the last rise, and the ruins of Santa Rosalia suddenly loomed close at hand ahead, almost buried in a jungle of untended fruit trees and wild pines and oaks that were reclaiming the lands that had been cleared. Wild lilac and roses were blooming. Mustard gilded the open stretches along the river. The massive, broken adobe walls lay silent in the sun, extending long shadows.

They tethered the team to a tree and moved into the walls. Tumblewoods were piled in corners. Sagebrush, manzanita and prickly-pear grew among the debris. Father O'Flaherty climbed over piles of rubble and entered the big oblong space of what had been the main church. The greater part of the roof had fallen, and if there had been pews they were gone now, used no doubt as firewood by settlers or for other purposes.

The padre crossed himself and knelt to pray. Dan stood there for a time, then found his way to open space beyond the ruins. He began circling Santa Rosalia, scanning the ground.

The padre joined him. "What are you looking for, my son?" he asked.

"I was wondering if anyone had ever dug outside the walls of the mission for this treasure," Dan said.

"Oh, yes," the padre said. "The ground was well turned over for years, but nothing was ever found. Brush has covered evidence of their efforts."

"Did the Coates brothers ever dig or drill around here?"

The padre eyed him. "I begin to see what you are driving at," he said. "I fear you are on the wrong track. I'm sure they did not. It would have been common knowledge. Everyone would have known they were not seeking water."

"Do you really believe there is such a treasure, Father?" Dan asked.

"I have seen some evidence," the padre admitted. "Among the Indians there are old curved daggers, ancient muskets with flared muzzles, and objects of gold and silver that were

140

obviously from heathen temples. I have seen them because I am a priest, and the tribes trust me. These things were handed down from the old ones."

"Were they found at Santa Rosalia?" Dan asked.

"Where else?"

"You say the pirates were jumped by the Indians and besieged until they were wiped out," Dan said. "Did it all happen right here at the mission?"

Again the padre eyed him. "No," he said slowly. "There was evidence of a running fight. Old knives, pistols, bullets, and such. Evidently the pirates were first attacked by Indians as they tried to escape from the basin, and were forced to retreat to the mission to make a stand."

Dan smashed a fist into a palm. "That's it!" he exclaimed. "That's the answer!"

"What do you mean?" Father O'Flaherty demanded.

Dan did not reply. He suddenly realized that the sun was long gone. Deep shadows were engulfing the basin. The latent uneasiness in him suddenly drove a chill through him.

"Let's go back!" he exclaimed. He hurried the puffing padre back to the sheep wagon, took over the reins himself, and startled the mules into a resentful trot.

Full darkness was settling as they came in sight of the Vickers' house. No light showed.

He left the wagon at a run. "Jennifer!" he shouted. "Mrs. Webb!"

There was no answer. He raced to the kitchen door which stood open. "Jennifer!" he shouted again. "Len!"

His words echoed emptily through the dark, unlighted house. The rooms were in great disorder. Chairs were overturned. A stand in the sitting room on which had stood a lamp with a garishly painted shade was overturned, the shade shattered. Spilled kerosene stained the carpet, its odor heavy in the air. The struggle had extended into the bedroom. A window was broken, evidently by a thrown chair.

The padre had followed Dan. Both of them stood appalled,

141

frozen by horror. Then Dan heard a small sound. It came from the bunkhouse. He raced through the kitchen and across the dogtrot. He found Lennie's lank length stretched out on the floor of the bunkhouse. He was gagged, his hands and ankles tightly bound with strips torn from bedding. He had an ugly gash on his forehead that extended into his hair, but the bleeding had stopped.

"He's alive!" Dan croaked. "Fetch some water, Father!"

He freed the gag and cut away the bonds. The padre brought water and used it to cool Lennie's forehead. Dan lighted the lamp. After a time Lennie began to respond. He moaned. His eyes finally fluttered and began to focus.

He recognized Dan and the padre. "What—where?" he moaned.

"You'll be all right, Len," Dan said. "What happened?"

"I—I don't know," the youth mumbled. "I came out of the kitchen door, an' somethin' hit me. All I remember was bright lights in my brain."

"Did ye see who did it, lad?" Father O'Flaherty asked.

"I didn't see nothin'," Lennie said.

"Do you remember about when it happened?" Dan asked.

Lennie tried to think. "The sun was jest goin' down," he finally decided. "I was goin' out to see if I could sight you comin' back."

Dan ran out of the house. A hundred yards away stood the brushy line of a side creek that reached the main river half a mile away. Cottonwoods, locusts, and willows grew thickly there. He raced to the line of brush. There was still enough afterlight so that he was able to locate a spot where horses had been tied up under heavy cover at a distance from the house. As best he could make out, there had been only two animals and they had been carrying heavy weights when they pulled out.

Dan ran back to the corral where Lennie had quartered the roan saddlehorse. He began rigging the animal with grim speed. Father O'Flaherty intercepted him as he started to swing into the saddle.

"What are you going to do, my son?" he asked.

"My God!" Dan said icily. "Why didn't I use my head? They were out there all the time, watching, waiting a chance. They must know we're on to them."

He tried to stir the horse into motion. "I'll send a doctor out to take a look at Lennie," he said.

Father O'Flaherty clung to his knee. "No! No! My son! You have a terrible look in your face. Do not take the law into your own hands. Vengeance is mine, saith the Lord. Do not . . ."

His voice faded under the blaze in Dan's eyes. "They've murdered men, even their own kind," Dan said. "Now they're going to murder women. They can't let them live to accuse them. You know that."

"You'll only die," the padre pleaded. "These are desperate men, dazzled by the hope of growing rich. You'll only be one against them. You don't even know who they are."

"I know," Dan said. "And so do you. I'll make someone tell what they've done with Bart Webb's wife—and mine."

"Find the sheriff," the padre urged. "This is the responsibility of the law. Honeywell will . . ."

He was talking to the wind. Dan slapped the roan and was on his way. Looking back he saw the padre making the sign of the cross and kneeling to pray.

He headed for Pinedale. He knew it was hopeless to attempt to trail his quarry. Whoever they were, they had at least a two-hour start, for all signs indicated they had moved in on the Vickers' house soon after he and the padre had headed for the mission.

He heard a rider coming up the trail in the same direction he was heading—coming very fast. He eased up on the roan and the rider overtook him. He was Bart Webb, on as big a mount as Dan had ever seen. The animal was lathered, almost winded. It had been driven to its limit.

Webb wore chaps, cuffs, and the jacket and battered hat of a man who had been popping the brush. He was armed with a holstered six-shooter and had a rifle in a sling on the saddle.

He came alongside Dan and seized the bridle of the roan, bringing both animals to a stop. Dan saw that he was clutching a small object in his hand. Peering close in the deepening darkness Dan saw that it was a heart-shaped gold locket, on a broken gold chain. He remembered that he had seen Consuelo Webb wearing the ornament.

"I found this hangin' on the gate of my corral when me'n the crew came in from roundin' up some beef to sell," Webb said hoarsely. "Where's my wife? Talk, man. Fast!"

"They've got her," Dan said.

Bart Webb snapped open the locket. It contained a small scrap of folded paper. Webb opened it and thrust it in Dan's face, but he could not make out the scrawled words in the fading light.

"It says that if I don't get out of the basin right away, the next thing they'll send me are my wife's fingers," Webb said hoarsely. "These devils who've been hounding me to pull out, have got her. Where's my niece? You know she's a Webb, don't you? You was supposed to guard her."

"They've got her, too," Dan said. "They must have been watching the Vickers' place and injuned in while the padre and me were down at the mission for a couple of hours."

"They're—they're dead?"

"Not yet at least," Dan said icily. "Have you had any water wells dug or drilled at your place in the last year or so?"

"Water wells? Are you crazy? What's that got to do with it?"

"Everything! Think, man! It's important!"

"We had a new well dug some time ago," Webb said hoarsely. "The old well was too shallow an' goin' dry. We wanted one nearer the house."

"Alex Coates did the job?"

Bart Webb peered closely at him. "Yeah," he said. "The

first try was a failure. Alex said they hit bedrock, so he dug on the far side of the house an' brought in good water."

"Who helped Alex?"

"Why, his brother, of course. Clem always helped Alex. He only drove stage in slack times."

"Was anyone else there when they hit the bedrock?" Dan demanded. "Willis Mason, maybe? Or Abel Jenkins?"

Bart Webb, confused, tried to think. "A lot o' folks stopped by to pass the time of day when they saw what was goin' on. Not Willis. Him an' me was still not exactly friendly. As fer Abel— Now that you mention it, I recollect that he did come by one day. Now why—?"

Dan had whirled his horse and was heading up the trail toward Pinedale. Bart Webb pursued him, and his big horse gamely responded and overtook the roan.

"Go back," Dan said. "Stay out of this!"

"What are you goin' to do?"

"Make somebody talk," Dan said.

Again Webb peered closely into Dan's face. "I'm beginnin' to see what this is all about. Do you think you can walk right in on people like that an' make 'em knuckle down? There'll be more than one."

"Go back," Dan repeated. "One of us has got to stay alive."

But the rancher kept forcing his horse on up the trail to Pinedale. The big animal's age began to tell, and it began to fall behind. Finally Dan was alone in the moonlight.

The roan was lathered also as he rode out of the scattered timber into the head of Pinedale's main street. The town was beginning to settle down for the night.

CHAPTER THIRTEEN

Dan rode down the center of the street, easing the roan to a walk. Many of the residences were already dark, their owners in bed. The mercantile was closed, the wide doors padlocked. Only half a dozen of the saloons and poker houses were lighted. The few pedestrians on the sidewalk paused, their eyes following the armed rider who passed by in silence.

A light burned in Abel Jenkins' office, but Dan continued on by. A few lights showed also in the big rambling home that Willis Mason occupied on the east fringe of town. Dan dismounted, leaving the roan ground-tied, walked up the curving path to the veranda and tried the gilded handle of the wide front door. The door was unlocked.

He entered the reception hall. The face of a black man appeared. He evidently was a servant who had been preparing for bed, for he was pulling up his suspenders. At his shoulder was the face of a black woman.

"Where's Mason?" Dan asked. He asked it quietly, but sudden terrible fright showed in the faces of the two servants. It was as though in the presence of this lean, tired man they also believed they stood in the presence of death.

"Mistah Mason ain't here," the black man quavered.

"How long has he been gone?"

There was no thought of evasion. "He ain't been home all day," the servant said. "Him an' Mistah Largo saddled up an' rode away this mawnin'."

Dan believed them. They were too frightened to lie. He left the house, mounted the roan, and returned into the commercial area of the town. He dismounted in front of Abel Jenkins' lighted office, walked to the door and tried the knob. The door was locked.

"Open up, Jenkins!" he said.

"Who are you?" Jenkins voice shrilled. "What do you want at this hour of the night?"

Dan backed off a pace and rammed the door with all his weight. The lock snapped and he hurled the door wide and entered. Abel Jenkins had been sitting at his desk, which was backed by filing cabinets, alongside of which the door to the rear was closed.

Jenkins started to rise. He made a motion toward an open drawer, where he evidently had a gun. He decided against it, letting his hand fall limply at his side. He gazed at Dan with eyes that were suddenly dull with the belief that he was about to die. His puffy face had turned the color of candle wax. His eyes darted to the closed door at the rear.

Dan spoke. "Where are they?"

"Where are who?" Jenkins replied, his voice a squeak.

Dan moved to the desk, reached over, caught the pudgy man by the front of his shirt. "I've got no time to spend on talk," he said. "Where did they take them?"

Jenkins tried feebly to resist, but Dan dragged him bodily across the desk, scattering papers and ledgers and spilling an inkstand.

"Slater!" Jenkins screeched. "Get him!"

The rear door was thrown open. The hard-faced Pete Slater was there, a brace of pistols in his hands.

"Kill him!" Jenkins gasped. "Kill him, Slater!"

Holding Jenkins with his left hand, Dan drew and fired from the hip. Both of Slater's guns exploded an instant late. They blew a great gust of powder smoke from the floor. Slater was hurled back by the smash of Dan's bullet into his chest. He fell groaning into the outer darkness.

Dan stood, his gun ready, in case more opponents appeared. But the door remained vacant. Dragging Jenkins with him, he backed through the front door into the street.

"Where are Consuelo Webb and my wife?" he asked.

Jenkins was limp with terror. "Let me go!" he begged.

"You were in on it," Dan said. "The Coates brothers hit the treasure while they were digging a well at the Webb ranch months ago. You happened to be there at the time. They covered up the hole they'd started, and dug a well somewhere else. You decided to take in Willis Mason as a partner, figuring he had the money and the brains to somehow get title to the Webb ranch so that you wouldn't have to share the treasure with anyone. The thing snowballed. Mason began posing as Bart Webb's friend while you and the Coates brothers terrorized settlers and blamed it on Bart Webb in order to stampede him into selling. You murdered the Coates brothers because they knew too much. You or Slater murdered Ed Vickers and Cal Sealover for the same reason. You stole that half a banknote that Willis Mason gave Sealover for trying to murder me and Jennifer Webb. But I had already seen it."

"Let me go!" was all that Abel Jenkins could repeat.

Bart Webb arrived on his exhausted horse. The catch-rope he had been using in the day's work was coiled on the saddle horn. Dan holstered his six-shooter. He slammed Abel Jenkins' face down in the dust, planted his boot on his back, and held him there squirming. He lifted the rope from Webb's saddle, shook out its length, and dropped the loop over Jenkins' head and shoulders, yanking it taut.

He mounted his horse and threw a loop of the rope around the horn, holding the free end.

"Where are they?" he asked again.

Jenkins appealed to Bart Webb. "Air you gonna let me be tortured?" he sobbed.

"You thief!" Dan said. "You murderer. It was you who killed Clem Coates with a pitchfork in Rimrock, hoping I'd be blamed for it—which I was. You were mixed up in the

149

murders of Ed Vickers and Cal Sealover. You planned it, even if your hired hands such as Alex Coates and Pete Slater probably fired the shots. Now you're in on the kidnaping of women, the worst crime in the book. Talk, man! Where did they take Consuelo and Jennifer Webb? You and Mason must have known from the first that she was Jennifer Webb. Where are they?"

"I don't know," Jenkins panted.

Dan kicked the roan into motion. Jenkins was dragged through the dust, his body jostling over wheel ruts. He grasped the rope desperately, trying to ease the violence.

"I tell you I don't know, Cameron," he gasped.

Dan yanked on the rope, turning the man a violent somersault in the street. "Where are Willis Mason and Max Largo?" he demanded.

Jenkins moaned through blood and shattered teeth. "Have pity, Cameron! I'm not a young man."

"Pity?" Dan answered. "For murder, for stealing women, for trying to have a man hung for a crime he didn't do? Talk, man! I'm asking you again where they took those women."

Jenkins moaned, "They'd kill me."

Dan threw his horse into a trot, dragging Jenkins along. Bart Webb, ashen-faced, followed on foot, walking like a man who was involved in a real-life nightmare.

"You devil!" Jenkins moaned. Dan urged the roan into a gallop. Jenkins screamed as his body bounced over wagon ruts. His clothes were being torn to shreds.

Dan swung off the road into rougher land. Cactus and rocks took toll of Jenkins. He again screamed, "Have pity."

"Where are they?" Dan asked again between set teeth. "You know, and I know you know."

"Stop!" Jenkins gasped. "Stop! I'll talk. It's the old mission. That's the place!"

Dan halted his horse. "The mission? Santa Rosalia? You're

lying. Father O'Flaherty and myself were there at the very time the women were kidnaped."

"It's the truth, so help me," Jenkins wailed. "That was the plan. The old wine vault at the east end of the old compound. That seemed a safe place."

Dan debated it for a space. He realized that it might have been possible. The kidnapers and their captives could have followed the cover of the river brush south of the wagon trail while keeping an eye on himself and the padre's sheep wagon, then could have moved into the ruins at dusk with the women. One of them could have delivered the locket at the Circle W before Webb and his crew had come in from the range.

"Were there any more in on it than Willis Mason and Max Largo?" Dan demanded.

"No," Jenkins mumbled.

Bart Webb was staring numbly. "But Willis Mason was my friend," he said unbelievingly. "The only one who stood up for me through all this."

"In public," Dan said. "Under the surface he was the brains back of all this. He was trying to maneuver you into selling title to the Circle W to him. He was playing for millions. That's what they say the treasure might be worth."

Bystanders had gathered, and were gaping in horror at Abel Jenkins. Sheriff Jim Honeywell arrived on foot, panting. He, too, stared incredulously. "Good Lord!" he croaked. "Is that really you, Abel? What in God's name is going on?"

Dan tossed him the end of the rope. "Drag him to your jail, Honeywell," he said. "He's involved in murders and the kidnaping of Consuelo Webb and my wife. And a lot of other things. Send the doctor out to the Vickers' place. Len Vickers has been slugged. The padre is with him but he needs looking after."

He looked at Bart Webb. "We both need fresh horses," he said. "We'll borrow them at the livery. Let's go."

They strode away, leaving Jim Honeywell standing there

gaping, holding the rope, with Abel Jenkins on hands and knees, animal-like, sobbing weakly.

They led their horses to the livery, picked fresh animals, and changed rigging swiftly. Bart Webb rode in silence as they headed away from Pinedale. It was Dan who broke that silence.

"Let me handle this," he said. "It's more in my line. All you'll do is get yourself killed, and maybe the ladies too."

"I'll be the judge of that," Bart Webb said. "It's the lives of my wife and my niece you're talking about."

"This marriage to Jennifer was a business arrangement at first," Dan said. "A matter of convenience. It's different now. If she doesn't come out of this alive I'll hunt down every man involved and make him pay."

They rode on with the moon painting fantastic shapes and shadows in the basin. The somber sawtooth bluffs looked down upon them. The fragrance of the cedars and pines was sweet and clean in the night.

They reached the Vickers' homestead, where lamplight showed. Father O'Flaherty came hurrying on foot down the side road to meet them.

"Sure an' Lennie is able to sit up an' take food," he said. "What news do you have of the ladies?"

"Pray for them," Dan said. "And for all of us."

He and Bart Webb rode on, leaving the padre standing there sorrowing and once more making the sign of the cross, then kneeling to pray.

Dan discovered that faint dawn was in the sky, so swiftly had the night evaporated in the stress of events. The moon was a pale and aging ghost.

Santa Rosalia finally appeared close at hand ahead, the fallen roofs catching the first warm glint of the coming day, the jagged, massive walls black and still holding the memory of the night.

They dismounted, leaving the horses at a distance. "The wine vault," Dan asked softly. "Do you know where it is?"

152

Bart Webb nodded and led the way. They moved slowly, carefully, circling the bulk of the broken walls, but their boots occasionally grated harshly on gravel and dry twigs.

Bart Webb crouched and breathed, "There!"

Daybreak was strengthening. Dan could make out the arched entrance to what evidently had been an underground vault. The space had been partly cleared of debris, evidently by treasure hunters, but the structure itself seemed fairly intact.

They both crouched there, instinctively trying to silence their breathing, although Dan was acutely aware that their arrival must surely be known to anyone who might be on vigil in the vault. If anyone was really there.

Dan thought, with sinking heart, that Abel Jenkins might have lied, led them on a false trail. He gazed at the lightening sky. The shadows were still pooled on the earth around him. They were his enemies now—allies of anyone who might be waiting in the deeper shadows of the black arched entrance.

"We'll wait for better light," he murmured. And sank down back of a heap of rubble. Bart Webb hesitated, then reluctantly followed that example. The rancher whispered huskily, "They're in there. I know it. I can feel it. Let's rush 'em."

"Better to make them come to us," Dan said. "Wait, I say!"

But the rancher could not be restrained. He lifted his voice. "Consuelo!"

The words seemed to echo in the silence and reecho. Dan clapped a hand over the rancher's mouth, even knowing that it was useless, for the damage, if any, had been done.

The silence seemed to hang, linger like a weight. Then Dan heard it. The faintest of sounds. It was a woman's voice who had attempted to cry out and had been silenced. But that was enough. He knew it had been Jennifer's voice. At least she was still alive.

There could be no more waiting for daylight, no more hoping for better odds. Dan lifted his own voice. "Come out, Mason! And you, Largo! It's over. You can't get away!"

A space of pulse-throbbing silence came, a space of no other sound at all. Then Willis Mason answered from the blackness. "Is that you, Bart, with Cameron?"

"It's me, Willis," Bart Webb said heavily. "You fooled me. I didn't realize you had sold your soul to the devil until Cameron forced the whole story out of Abel Jenkins tonight. Is my wife there—alive?"

"Here and alive," Mason said. "And in my arms. I'm coming out. I'll have Consuelo in front of me. Largo has your niece. I knew from the day she arrived who she was and why she was posing as a settler. I tried to spook her into leaving, but she hung on and now she will be Max's shield. Yes, Max is here with me. I suppose Abel told you that, also. We'll take them with us as long as they're needed. All we want is time. We've got horses tied up out there. We intend to have a chance to get away. We're coming out. Is it a deal?"

"Come out," Dan said.

"He's lying," Bart Webb breathed. "They're giving in too easy. He only intends to use the women as shields so that he and Largo can shoot us down and get away."

"It's the only way," Dan murmured. He spoke louder. "Come out anytime, Mason."

"Don't make any mistakes, Cameron," Mason answered. "You went through something like this once before, I understand. Do you want another innocent girl to die for you?"

Consuelo spoke, her voice showing the hoarseness of having been gagged. "Do not believe them, *querido mío*. They only intend to kill us all. They have gone too far. They have lost, but all they hope for now is to save their own lives."

Her voice was choked off, evidently by a hand. But Jennifer spoke shrilly. "She is right, Cameron. They only want to kill you and—"

She also was violently silenced. "You little fool!" Max Largo's voice snarled. "I ought to—"

He left it unfinished. There was another space of silence. Dan could hear Bart Webb's labored breathing at his side.

Then Willis Mason spoke again. "Stay where you are, Cameron. And you, Bart. We can see you plainly, see any move you try to make. We're coming out. Put your hands in the air."

Dan lifted his arms and Bart Webb reluctantly followed suit. Max Largo spoke to Mason. "Watch Cameron. He's fast. He's greased lightning."

Shapes emerged from the maw of the vault. The first was Largo. He had Jennifer gripped tight against him, his left hand clamping her waist, his right hand holding a cocked pistol.

Willis Mason followed, half carrying Consuelo Webb, being very careful to keep her body as a shield. The hair of both captives had fallen loose and floated in the first touch of the morning breeze.

Consuelo spoke. "Shoot! Shoot this devil through my body. It is the only way to kill a demon, *querido mío.*"

Then Max Largo fired. He meant to kill Dan. Dan had known this was coming. It was the only course Largo and Willis Mason could follow. Jennifer must have sensed the moment also and had moved. Largo's bullet scored Dan's left arm.

He was moving to upset Largo's aim. His six-shooter was in his hand, leveled. He crouched there with only Largo's head visible above Jennifer's shoulder. Searingly in his memory was that moment on the steps of the little church on the Wyoming plains when the girl he had loved had died for him in his arms.

Now Jennifer was that girl and he might kill her instead of Largo. Jennifer again took a hand. She screamed and burst into frenzied activity, kicking and struggling.

Largo was off balance. His head was still clear in spite of his attempts to quiet his captive. It was a small target in light that was still pale and uncertain.

Dan fired. Max Largo must have realized that he was a dead man, must have known that he had signed his death warrant when Jennifer began struggling. Dan's bullet struck him between the eyes. Largo's gun exploded, but the shot went wild. There was on his lips a pleading word that Dan did not understand. It was as though Max Largo was asking for another chance—another chance to kill.

Largo then muttered, "No! Oh, no!" Then he pitched to the ground, dead.

Dan crouching, whirled, swinging his gun on Willis Mason, who clutched Consuelo tighter against him as a shield.

"I'll kill her!" Mason croaked. "Stand back or I'll blow out her brains. Let me go and she won't be hurt."

He was still lying. He knew it, Bart Webb knew it. The festering jealousy of a lost love, of a lost fortune, was in Mason's voice now, denying his words.

Bart Webb moved toward them. "Stand back!" Mason screamed. Consuelo fought with tigerish strength. She tore away from Mason's grasp and pitched to her knees, leaving her husband to face Willis Mason. Guns were in both of their hands.

"I've always hated you!" Mason babbled, and fired. The range was almost point blank, but Consuelo had hurled herself at the man's knees in time, staggering him, and the bullet went wide of the mark.

Bart Webb fired a single shot, and Dan could see the savage force of the slug as it smashed into and through Willis Mason's body. The man crumbled, and fell on his face, writhing there alongside the body of Max Largo, which was already stilling in the complete finality of death.

Dan lowered his six-shooter. Once more he had been forced to kill, but he had been spared the taking of Willis Mason's life at least.

And Jennifer was still alive. His bullet must have missed her only by inches. He began to shake as the enormity of what it might have been came upon him.

He walked to her and it was she who took him into her arms, comforting him, for she knew the terrors that racked him. "My darling," she murmured. "Oh, my darling. It's all over. Over forever." She kissed him tenderly.

Consuelo was clinging to Bart Webb. He was stroking her hair, trying to comfort her, telling her how wonderful life was going to continue to be with her.

Hoofbeats sounded. Men from Pinedale were arriving, with the burly figure of Jim Honeywell in the lead.

It was late afternoon and the sun was once more sinking toward the rim of the escarpment to the west. The Circle W ranch was a madhouse. The entire population of Pinedale seemed to have arrived.

The treasure had been found. It had been dug up under the direction of Jim Honeywell and Father O'Flaherty. It lay on tables and chairs and on the floor in the main room of the Webb ranch house, the doors guarded by armed men. Gold coins of exotic mint and undefined value were there in stacks and spilling from rotting chests and the leather bags that had held them. There were chalices of gold, studded with gems, and images of silver and gold. Pearls, emeralds, rubies.

"Much of it is holy," Father O'Flaherty had said. "Taken from churches of my faith. I claim such of it as is fitting in the name of the church."

"Take it all," Bart Webb had said. "It's evil. It's dead men's wealth. It should have been left where it was—in the earth along with the men who died for it, along with those who killed to try to hold it. Take it all."

"That will be up to the state," Jim Honeywell had said. "After all, Bart, it was found on your land. The law will decide."

Dan sat in a small bedroom away from the confusion. His injured arm had been doctored and was in a sling. Honeywell had taken depositions, which would be read whenever the inquest was held. The verdict was not in doubt.

He had not seen anyone in some time. He was at the end
of his rope, mentally and spiritually. He was alone and very
lonely.

Consuelo entered. She came to him as he got to his feet and
kissed him. "Come!" she said. "Everything is ready!"

He followed her, not understanding. She led him through
the rambling ranch house and out by way of a rear door. A
ranch wagon stood there with a team in harness. The canvas
top was decorated with wildflowers and strings of handmade
pompoms in gay colors. The horses sported cockades. The
wheels were gay flower patterns. Women of the town and
basin stood in the background smiling. Some had tears on
their cheeks.

Jennifer sat on the seat of the wagon. She was garbed in
white silk, and her slippers were of white satin. She had on
elbow-length white gloves and a dreamy bridal veil floated in
the faint breeze. Her garb was a fashion of another day, but it
was devastating in its beauty.

"I'm sorry it is not a golden chariot with white chargers in
harness," Consuelo said. "Bless you, Daniel, and be happy forever. You will live in peace now. I will pray for that."

Dan dazedly mounted the seat of the vehicle. Jennifer spoke
demurely. "Please be careful, my husband, as you drive. I am
timid about such things."

"Where do you want to go?" Dan asked.

"To heaven," she answered. She leaned against him, very,
very tightly against him. She repeated it again, softly, "To
heaven tonight, and for a lifetime, my husband."

Dan stirred the horses into motion.